Mud, Men and Machines

A collection of short stories written by a Geologist

Alan Watchman

Other novels by Alan Watchman:

The Ice Cream Killings

Secrets at Hanging Rock

No Time for Tears

Yarraman Gold

Solstice at Flinders Cove

Serpent Salt

Love in War

268: The mystery of a Parmigianino oil painting

The Gilgunnia Girl

Run from Coromandel

Where Rocks Cry

Horner's Bridge

Ripples on the River

Once, Twice, Thrice

The Apstein Enigma

Dead Skin

Edith & Grace: Journey to Melbourne 1941

Somebody Knows

The Indispensable Man

Take a bucket and fill it with water,

Put your hand in it up to your wrist;

Pull it out and the hole that remains,

Shows how much you would be missed.

From Saxon White Kessinger, 1959.

Contents

Characters

Tom Waterhouse	Perth Geologist, friend of the author
Ailsa	school teacher, friend of Tom's, Darwin
Phil Mcleod	field assistant, Darwin
Dillon	bush mechanic, field assistant, Darwin
Dick and Mary	English couple, Darwin
Jocelyn	school teacher, friend of Tom's, Darwin
Andy Brown	friend of Jocelyn's
Kathleen, Darrell	friends of Jocelyn's
Charlie Simpson	elderly Québec resident, Canada
Bonnie Devine	owner/manager Cheminis Lodge, Canada
Dave French	assistant, Cheminis Lodge, Canada
Matthew	CEO Origino Pty Ltd
Dashkar	driver, Origino
Jerry	geologist, Gobi Coal and Energy Pty Ltd
Armac	driver, Gobi Coal and Energy
Sirchin	retired geologist, consultant to Origino
Sumiya	young Mongolian geologist
Bajig	Sumiya's cousin,
Choi	Mongolian geology student
Kulan	female drilling camp cook
Ganana	Kulan's male assistant
Bargii	fire worker, Mongolia
Natasha Yevtushenko	Intourist Guide, USSR.

Warning signs in Ulaanbaatar.

WARNING: Some readers may find the contents of this book offensive because of the coarse language, swear words, sexual references and use of inappropriate expressions it contains. While working in remote localities there is a strong tendency for the language of men to degrade. I am not condoning the issue simply stating a well known fact. Each reader will react according to their own standards. You have been warned.

Dillon

Dillon was not his real name, but given to him by his Darwin mates. I first met Dillon when he signed up as the mechanic on a field crew we assembled for a mapping expedition into Arnhem Land in northern Australia. Dillon's qualifications did not include 'mechanic', but odd jobs man. He could turn his hand to anything and fix any machine, he said. He was right! He rolled his own cigarettes; Drum tobacco. Being frugal he kept the butts and later mixed the remnants with new tobacco for a 'hit', he said. He wore shorts and a dark singlet, but no shoes; his feet were brown, hard, the soles like leather.

One occasion when Dillon's skills came in handy was during a week I spent with him mapping in the area around the King River. We either drove Toyota or Land Rover four wheel drive vehicles, and this week it was a short wheel base Land Rover. Typically, we headed out from the base camp on Monday morning loaded with camping gear, radio phone, water and food for a week. A field assistant drove the geologist, in this case, me around to examine exposures of rocks previously identified from the study of aerial photographs. In those days, the 1970s, GPS units had not been invented. Navigation was therefore by map and air photograph. Dillon was my driver for the week.

We drove for almost one day before we ran into our first problem. As we mounted a ridge in four wheel drive we heard a loud bang from the front axle and then the speed of the vehicle dropped to a crawl. Dillon stopped to look for the problem; maybe just a stick jammed in the drive shaft. I sat in the vehicle looking at my air photos to see where we were. Bad news! Dillon reported several teeth on the crown and pinion of the front-wheel drive had broken. He would have to disconnect the drive and then only have two-wheel drive for the rest of the week. No problems for Dillon; he simply got out his tool box and removed the pinion from the crown wheel assembly and once it was out we saw where two adjacent teeth had snapped off the wheel.

I should have explained before. We drove across country, not on roads because there were few dirt tracks in the region. We made our own track by picking a way through rocks, around stumps and fallen logs and down into creeks and up the other sides. In four-wheel drive this is relatively easy, but the hazard of only two-wheel drive is becoming stuck in sand or at the bottom of a creek is highly likely unless care is taken selecting the route and in preparing the track. We surveyed each creek crossing and spent time to corduroy the path by breaking shrubs and laying branches, rocks and logs across the sandy creek bottom so we would have good traction and could maintain speed down and up the other side. We picked a steep entry into a crossing and a shallow exit so it was easy to traverse a dry stream bed without getting stuck.

The next day as we drove much more carefully through the bush we took our time selecting the way we went. We always took precautions so we did not have to push our way out of a sandy bog. Our other problem we realised immediately the teeth on the crown wheel had snapped was we did not have a winch to pull ourselves out of situations if we did become stuck.

Fortunately, on another occasion with Dillon we were in a Toyota with a winch. Then, he drove too close to the damp edge of a salt flat and we did get bogged in wet mud. The winch cable was just long enough to reach a small tree on the rocky edge of the depression and we pulled ourselves out. Without a winch we would have had to dig and rock the vehicle back and forth while quickly placing sticks or rocks under the wheels.

We were not having much luck. Bush driving inevitably involved knocking down small trees and bushes with the risk a hard branch will penetrate the radiator. You guessed it; a stick went into the radiator and the engine started to overheat. Dillon spotted the sudden rise in temperature and stopped. It was not just one stick. Three holes were visible in the radiator.

This was a small problem for Dillon as he decided he could fix it simply. He walked to the back of the vehicle and got out a pot, flour and other ingredients. I had to ask him why he was making a dumpling mix. Was he hungry? No. Too early for lunch! He said he was making up his dumpling mix, but not to eat. Intrigued, I watched. He stopped briefly to roll a cigarette, lit it and continued his repair work. Now Dillon's dumplings are something else. They certainly fill a stomach, like a lead weight, and eating two at breakfast satisfies hunger all day. He had other cooking skills I found out later!

The mix he made comprised flour, milk, molasses and panel beater's putty, which he quickly whipped up and poured into the radiator before he added water and got me to start the engine. As water leaked out he added more of his concoction. The leak decreased and finally stopped. Then he boiled the billy and made tea.

Breakfast with Dillon in the bush was interesting. He boiled water and made either hard boiled eggs or poached eggs in the boiling water. As a good conservationist and saving hot water he then used the same water to pour into a mug and add a tea bag or instant coffee. He just fished out any floating bits of egg before handing me the cup!! No wonder I thought the tea tasted strange on the first morning.

We had some issues with our camp cook and the boss fired him. Without a cook in camp on weekends Dillon offered his services. He can do anything, so he can certainly cook. Right! Well, I'm not so sure. He made a curry of beef and vegetables with chilli to spice it up. A cigarette hung out of his mouth while cooking and smoke occasionally stung his eye. Ash intermittently dropped into the mix; he just looked around to see if anyone noticed, smirked, then continued what he was doing. He served the meal beaming with pride and returned to get his own plate. One mouthful was enough to send me rushing in pain to the water cart as sweat poured into my burning eyes. After I had splashed water on my face and swallowed several mouthfuls to cool my burning tongue I struggled back into the mess where everyone else tentatively picked at their plates.

Dillon was explaining his recipe because he did not know what went wrong. He had chopped the meat into bite sized pieces, cut up onions, carrots and potatoes, and thrown in two cans of peas. There was nothing wrong with it or so I thought. How wrong can a bloke be? Why was there a sharp burning pain in my eyes? It's a curry, right, so according to Dillon to spice it up bird's eye chillies should be added. Ok, I can tolerate chilli. How many? Well, according to Dillon's calculation, twenty! Even he could not eat his curry despite his attempt with milk, beer and water to wash it down. It would have killed a dog if we had one!!

The rest of the week was uneventful except for two flat tyres Dillon repaired one night. We always carried spare tyres and repair kits. We made slow progress mapping and did not take any chances crossing dry stream beds. Friday afternoon we headed back towards base camp. One last dry creek to cross and then we would find the graded track and make it easy to drive into our base camp. I looked forward to taking a shower, the first of the week. The creek had steep banks on both sides. We patrolled along the winding drainage looking for a suitable place to cross. The only place we found was the opposite of what we needed. It had a shallow entry and steep exit, up a sharp slope. Could we run the vehicle fast enough across the sandy flat and up the rise in two wheel drive? No! We tried several times, but could not make it up the final few metres. We made a corduroy of branches and sticks across the sandy bottom, so we could go faster before racing up the opposite bank, but still no luck making the crossing.

Our plan was to boil the billy and wait for sundown when we could use the radio and call the camp to tell them our location and ask for another vehicle to come and tow us out. We had a few hours to kill. After the billy boiled and we drank our tea we sat under the shade of a tree. Lizards played in the fallen leaves. Black ants crawled across the sand. March flies landed and were swatted. We talked.

Dillon told me his history. He told me of his time in jail. He had spent fifteen years locked up because he had killed a man in a drunken fight in a Darwin bar. His nickname was not just Dillon, but Killa Dillon. He'd forgotten to tell us that, he said, a gaping hole evident in his teeth as he smiled.

He had just finished his lengthy story when we thought we heard a putt putting sound, wafting in and out on the breeze. We stood and climbed the bank to listen and look for the cause of the noise. In addition to the increasing engine noise we heard chattering, voices. Then we saw it making a trail of dust. A tractor towing a trailer loaded with boys. They were heading to the community centre for a ceremony. After a quick chat they unhitched the trailer and using a chain they carried for just such purposes, the tractor hauled our vehicle up the last few metres of the bank. We thanked them and headed back to camp.

An eventful week it certainly was and one I'll never forget. Now Killa Dillon only kills snakes and magpie geese. He grows mangoes on his farm. I thank my lucky stars, and everyone else should too, he never opened a restaurant.

The problem with Phil

In Arnhem Land, a prominent pinnacle of sandstone stands above the surrounding flood plain and tall savannah forest providing a landmark for many kilometres. From a westerly perspective, approaching by corrugated dusty reddish road it forms a spectacular phallic shape while from the south a sensitive eye imagines a proud head and face, a woman on his back. Carved out by tropical erosion throughout millennia the rock became a sacred place for Aboriginal people. In painful ceremonies, young boys took their first initiation steps to manhood.

Nearby and adjacent to trickling Cooper Creek, Europeans had erected a geological base camp, a temporary cluster of brown and green tents fringing an elliptical waterhole framed by Pandanus and tall paperbark trees. Freshwater crocodiles and black brim swam in the clear deep water sharing its tranquillity with the team of geologists and their crew of assistants, mechanic and cook who occupied the camp.

Every Monday morning was hectic. Usually a geologist and his field assistant hurried to set off on their week long mapping expedition. They packed food supplies, water and field gear in the yellow and white four-wheel drive vehicle. On the passenger seat, the black bearded geologist put a collection of air photographs, which he would use for navigation, his notebooks, pens, Chinagraph pencils, erasers and compass. In the back of the vehicle, on top of a large, unpainted metal trunk and a spare tire his sluggish assistant stowed sleeping swags of green canvas with rolled bedding and mosquito netting, and two cloth bags filled with changes of clothes. The metal trunk contained additional supplies; tinned meat, braised steak and onions, peas, beetroot, cake, rice cream, milk, and soup; essential items for when they emptied the Esky cooler. Depending on preferences, usually dictated by the assistant, the cooler held steaks, eggs, lettuce, tomatoes, bread, juice and most importantly four frozen cans of beer. Another box had onions, garlic, carrots and potatoes. In a crate wrapped in dishcloths and sealed inside plastic containers to keep out the dust were assorted cooking pots, a fry pan, utensils, a blackened billy can, cutlery and coloured metal plates and bowls.

The day before the field assistant had checked the vehicle. He measured the tire pressures, and looked for tire damage, ensured the engine oil level was correct, inspected the battery fluid, filled the vehicle with petrol from the hand-operated pump on one of the many tilted drums in the fuel dump and topped up the long-range water tank from the water hole. The two men relied entirely on the vehicle to transport them through the rugged terrain, across steeply entrenched dry creeks and over rocky slopes. It had to be roadworthy and well maintained otherwise their lives would be in peril. The radio and aerial would be their only communication link with the world for the next four days, so the geologist double-checked the equipment worked before installing it in a wooden box alongside the metal bin.

Tom Waterhouse, the bearded geologist noticed Phil Macleod, his assistant was subdued. He wondered why Phil was slower this morning, but knew he had plenty of time to find out why, so he never said anything, just continued with his packing. Tom was a geologist from Perth, about 183 cm tall, strongly built, and now tanned from several weeks of regular exposure to the daily dry season sun. He wore tan shorts and shirt, and robust black boots. His dark curly hair and beard were uncombed and long. His assistant, Phil would drive the vehicle. Phil was about 178 cm, clean-shaven, heavily built with a large protruding beer gut, which hung expectantly over an engraved brown leather belt. He wore no boots. His hardened soles were like lightweight boots on the sandy soil. In rocky areas, he reluctantly put on boots he kept in the back of the vehicle. One wide swath of thin brown hair usually swept back from his forehead, but today his hair was uncombed and he looked dishevelled. His shirt hung out of his crumpled shorts. His red veined eyes replaced the usual pair of bright brown ones that caught every movement. His face had stubble. Tom knew something had changed in Phil over the weekend, but he had other things on his mind and he would talk with Phil once they left camp.

When Tom had finished organising his gear, he walked to the large square brown tent alongside a longer one, where they cooked and ate their meals on weekends. Entering the tent, he told his boss, Campbell Macgregor he was almost ready to set out from camp. Macgregor, a graduate from Edinburgh University also intended leaving camp after attending to mail and other administrative matters. Macgregor was encouraging the third geologist, Roger Peterson to get a move on and leave camp too. Roger was in the tent still preparing his air photographs and organising his field notebooks and maps. He had not prepared anything over the weekend, but had taken a leisurely weekend to spend with his wife. They stayed in a caravan at one end of the camp, a hundred metres away from the mess tent. His assistant, John was busily preparing their vehicle and supplies before they too would leave for another area.

Each geologist had specific areas within the larger region to cover by vehicle and foot so they could record the nature of the rocks, cropping out. Together they would update the existing and poorly detailed geological map of the region. An exploration company had found uranium and the government wanted to produce a much better map to assist with understanding the mineralisation.

Tom saw Roger and Macgregor were at logger heads again and quickly said he was leaving. He and Phil said their farewells telling Macgregor they were heading to Black Rock, a large outlying sandstone massif about thirty kilometres north of camp. They would be back the following Friday afternoon as usual. They climbed into their vehicle and slowly headed out of camp to the Gove Road along a single vehicle track that wound snake-like between lofty grey-white paperbark and dark stringy bark and Woollybutt trees. Gove Road running from east to west across Arnhem Land linked several Aboriginal communities and outstations, and provided access to the region during the dry season. From November to March, the wet season, the road was impassable. Dry sandy creek beds became gushing torrents of deep swirling muddy water. Clay soils turned slippery and bogged many vehicles endeavouring to navigate the route.

When they reached the Gove Road, they turned west without any words between them and continued along the dusty graded route towards the intersection with another track that went north to the Cobourg Peninsula and Fort Wellington on Raffles Bay. The Fort was the second unsuccessful attempt by Europeans to settle in northern Australia. Little remains of the fort as the military outpost lasted less than two years before another unsuccessful settlement at Port Essington led to the founding of Darwin.

Phil tried focusing on both his driving and his physical condition, but his headache and churning stomach distracted him and affected his usually impeccable performance behind the wheel. Mistiming several gear changes at low engine revolutions and almost stalling at an easy dry creek crossing reminded Phil how unwell he was feeling. He was off his best and Tom knew it too, but Tom was preoccupied thinking about the mail John had brought back from Darwin.

Tom's brother was planning to marry a girl he had met the year before and had invited Tom to attend the ceremony. Tom's dilemma was he was in a remote bush camp and felt he would not be able to take leave for a week just to go to the wedding. He would have to think of another reason to justify travelling back to Darwin and then to Adelaide where the wedding was to be held. He had also received another letter from a woman who had started writing regularly to him from Canberra. He had only met her a month before he left

Canberra and he was not sure what he was going to write back. He realised his lack of experience with women would make it difficult for him to write back. What could he say? Tell her about the camp and his work. She would really like to know, he thought sarcastically. Tom had no idea and just pondered his options, including not answering. That might be best because he would be working out here for another three months. He hoped she would stop writing – save him the trouble of answering.

His brain quickly returned to the present as the vehicle bounced sharply over a hole in the road, the impact rocking the car sideways and knocking his head against the door frame. Phil would normally have missed it he thought. What had happened and why was Phil in this condition? Should he raise the issue or just wait for Phil to tell him what was wrong? He tried not to think about it. He looked out the window absentmindedly as they weaved through the forest and out onto a plain where two bush turkeys took flight, then back into more thick timber. He noticed the bumping and bouncing of the vehicle was less than usual as Phil was driving much slower than usual. What was wrong with Phil? Tom deliberated on the possibilities: hangover, stomach bug, bad news in a letter or just tiredness.

They reached a road junction and their turning point to the Cobourg Peninsula. The track widened out in a space cleared by many previous vehicles stopping there. Phil slowed the vehicle and then stopped. They had not spoken since leaving camp and now Tom looked at Phil and asked.

"What's up Phil, you don't seem your usual self today?"

Phil turned. He looked pale, tired and sickly. His eyes were bloodshot and sleepy. Glancing sheepishly at Tom, then lowering his head he replied wearily. "I'm crook."

"Why didn't you tell me before we left camp? We could have stayed there today."

"Too embarrassing."

"Why?"

Phil did not answer, but turned the engine off. He undid his seat belt and opened the car door. "I need a drink," he said tiredly. He reached onto the back seat and taking out a water bottle took a large swig. Almost instantly, Phil vomited violently. Tom stared still strapped in his seat. After several violent body-wrenching upheavals, Phil was able to stand up. He drank some more from his water bottle and spat the liquid out. A smirk appeared on Tom's face. Phil saw it and said, "It's not bloody funny you bastard."

Tom laughed. "Of course it is, you silly bugger. What in the hell were you doing last night?"

Phil walked around to the front of the car taking deep gulps of air into his lungs. His protruding belly heaving in and out, as though it were a large balloon expanding and contracting as air sucked in and blew out. He took another swig from the bottle, rinsed his mouth and then spat a long stream onto the dusty track. The water splashed and darkened the red clay soil. He coughed and spat a dollop of phlegm onto the dirt. Phil sucked air slowly into his lungs then blew it out noisily through pursed lips.

"Shit, I feel crook. That bloody Dillon has got a lot to answer for," he said disparagingly.

"The bastard said it would be alright and John agreed."

"What would be alright?"

Phil then, in fits and starts as his lungs and stomach would allow, related his story of the night before. He said it all started when John, another field assistant had returned to camp from Darwin on Sunday afternoon after he had gone there to buy supplies. He also came back with a small packet of marijuana. John liked to smoke and try different drugs, but the boss had employed him despite a government regulation against hiring people who took drugs.

That Sunday night, like most other nights before returning to the work of driving their vehicles on traverses through the bush the three field assistants sat around drinking beer and chatting. Dillon was a local Darwin man who had shot crocodiles, hunted buffaloes, farmed mangoes and worked as a stockman on a Vestey Ranch. He was the mechanic as well as a driver. John was Irish and had worked as a French teacher in a private school in London before venturing across the Middle East and Asia, finally landing broke in Darwin. He needed the driving work to get money so he could travel to Sydney, his final destination. Phil was also a local lad, but unlike Dillon, had trained as a draftsman and got a job as a junior cartographer with the government. In the dry season, he volunteered to be a field assistant so he could explore the bush. They had almost finished a case of VB between them when John mentioned he had some 'weed'. Did they want to try it?

Dillon rolled his own cigarettes, but Phil did not smoke. Neither had tried marijuana. John went to his tent and came back with a small plastic bag filled with dried green flowers, stalks and leaves. He rolled a joint, lit it with a match and showing the others how to smoke it took a drag. He passed the joint to Dillon who inhaled a short sharp breath. Dillon coughed and wheezed. Phil was unsure about trying it, but he was in the mood to try anything. John said it would be fine if he just took a drag. Dillon took another drag on the joint and blew out a jet of blue smoke. He convinced Phil there was nothing wrong with a couple of puffs, so Phil sucked on the joint.

"I didn't feel anything," Phil explained. "It just smelt different to tobacco smoke, that's all. We passed the joint around and getting more confident, I took deeper and deeper drags. That was fuckin' stupid. It made me relax, but nothing really happened. I thought I might hallucinate or faint, but I was fine last night when I went to bed. I guess it's the combo of the booze and the grass making me sick today. Dunno, maybe it's the coupla beers I had after the smoke."

Tom sensed this was not the real reason why Phil was crook. Just smoking dope after a couple of beers was nothing. He had never tried it himself, but he had heard other people describing the effects of marijuana and feeling crook was not one of them. There was something else wrong with Phil. Tom grunted and slid from the car to take a leak.

Phil continued, blaming his mate Dillon for his condition. "I hope Dillon is as crook as me. The bastard!"

The two men silently resumed their journey north. Meanwhile, back in camp, Macgregor told Dillon, much to his great delight they would leave camp tomorrow because he had to respond to administrative matters. Unsteadily Dillon returned to his tent and slipped into his bed to sleep off the combined effects of the alcohol and drugs. John unpacked the Esky putting his supplies back into the kerosene-operated refrigerator because the third geologist would also not leave camp until the next day. John took a cold beer from the fridge reefed the ring-pull open and took his medicine – the hair of the dog.

Tom kept thinking about Phil and surmised it was not just the grog and the dope. Maybe John had brought him a letter from Darwin with bad news. He wondered how he could get Phil to talk about the real problem troubling him: it had to be related to family, a girl friend, his job, money or health issues. Tom guessed Phil's problem was probably his girl friend. Was she pregnant?

"You know Phil; we're good mates aren't we?" Tom said after they had travelled a few kilometres along the edge of a black soil floodplain and through stands of paperbark. Phil grunted.

"I'd tell you if I were having a hard time about something," Tom continued. "You know that's what friends are for, aren't they? They listen and give advice and support. So, if there is anything troubling you, I'd listen and see if I could help. I don't want you to feel like you're alone with no one to share your problems with."

"I'm just crook," Phil said."Yeah you might be, but there's something else: something you haven't told anyone about."

Tom waited for his words to sink in. Phil was trying to avoid some deep buffalo wallows and trees. He misjudged a turn, grazed a tree and then went jarringly into a hollow.

"Stop the car!" Tom shouted.

Phil obeyed and looked at Tom.

"Look Phil. Your driving is up to shit today. I know you are crook, but you are also thinking about something else and it's affecting your concentration. Tell me what is on your mind or I'll drive back to camp and report you to Macgregor."

Phil unbuckled his seat belt and got out of the car. Unsteadily he stepped to the edge of the road.

"Gotta take a piss," Phil said.

Tom got out the car and taking his time to allow Phil to empty his bladder in private sauntered around to the driver's side of the car and leant against the bull bar. Phil turned back to the car and doing up his fly said in a quivering voice.

"Well, there is something." Gazing to the horizon across the shimmering flood plain as if looking for a landmark, Phil said. "It's me mate, Ray. He's dying. His wife wrote to me. John brought me the letter yesterday."

"I thought it was something like that," Tom said sympathetically.

Phil did not hear what Tom had said, he was preoccupied thinking about Ray. He continued as though Tom had not said anything. "Reading it in Fay's letter killed me. He's only got weeks to live she said. I won't see him before he dies. We've been mates since school: done everything together. Shit I feel crook. I need a drink."

While Phil reached into the back of the vehicle to get a drink Tom said, "Shit Phil, that's bad. Why didn't you tell Dillon and John last night instead of getting on the piss? They could have helped. You should have told me this morning and I would have asked Macgregor to give you a few days off so you could go into town."

After pausing to consider what Phil might be thinking, Tom added, "What's Ray dying of anyway?"

"Pancreatic cancer. Inoperable, Fay said."

"Bloody hell! That changes everything. You just have to get to town this weekend. Tell you what we'll do," Tom said thinking up a quick solution. "We'll do our work as soon as we can and head back to camp on Friday morning. You can switch with Dillon. He's supposed to go, but you can swap with him. Then drive into town Friday arvo and see Ray. I'll talk with Macgregor on the radio tonight and arrange it. What do you reckon?"

"Can you do that?"

"Sure. Consider it done. Now shift your arse and I'll drive."

The Diviner

The ferocious sun so searing the dark rocks were too hot to touch. Black shale, dolerite and basalt littering the featureless plain radiated oscillating heat waves upwards into my face compounding the unbearable burning sunlight. In the shimmering heat I saw a moving mirage approaching. While the object was at a distance I could not discern whether the vision was a camel, horse or human, but as it came nearer I saw its distinctive human shape.

I was in this wilderness surveying for a new railroad that would link Alice Springs to Darwin. A human apparition appearing from the desert was unexpected, particularly on such an unpleasant day. As I watched I detected its strangeness, an oddity about the human form as its shape developed a sharper outline with the decreasing shimmering interference. At first I could not figure what the oddity was; heatstroke, fever! I drank another mouthful of water to stop dehydrating and hallucinating.

The shimmering shape came closer and I saw a man beneath a wide-brimmed hat that provided much needed shade, matching mine. 'What in the hell is he doing out here,' I wondered. His gait was unusual, and that's what had caught my attention. When humans walk our arms swing back and forth, the left arm in time with the right foot and the left foot with the right arm, but his stride was different and his arms were not swinging. Instead, I saw his hands were clenched in fists out in front of his torso as if preparing for a fight. 'What's this guy up to?' I thought.

When he was about twenty metres from me he dropped his hands to his sides and walked normally. Then I saw he carried two thin wire objects in his hands."G'day," he said, transferring one of the objects from his right hand to his left. "Hot! Got any water to spare?"

I returned his greeting and took a bottle of water from the back seat of my four-wheel drive and handed it to him. He looked hard at me, but didn't say anything, his thirst obvious by the long gulps he took from the bottle."Thanks. Needed that. Left my bottle in the car. Stupid on a day like this, eh! Think it'll rain?" He smirked."No. No, chance of that. Thin clouds. Too high."He grunted, took another swig of water and asked."What're you doing here?""Could ask you the same thing," I replied before I thought of something more intelligent to say.

Then I told him my business checking on the survey route for the new railroad. He showed interest as soon as I started to explain. "Thought you might be," he said lifting the bottle to his lips again to drain the remaining liquid. "When's the train coming through?""Year or two. Depends. Money is the issue. Bloody bankers can't decide. Plans been drawn for a year now, but they hesitate. Think it's risky, they do. Procrastinating politicians are not much better. One says it's great – he's from Darwin, but others from Melbourne and Sydney think it's a waste of tax payers' money.""They should know about wasting tax payers' money. I think it's great. That's why I'm here."

We both kicked the ground, thinking what to say next.He raised the bottle, then saw it was empty. "Want another?" I said before he could ask."No, she'll be fine. I'll head back to my truck up the track a ways. Got some there.""And what are you doing here?" I asked as he turned to go."Prospecting. Looking for copper 'n gold.""What are those you've got there," I said pointing to the thin objects in his hand. They were two wires, like hard fencing wire that were bent to look like the letter 'L'."Rods. My divining rods.""How do they work?"

He hesitated, looked at me sideways as if assessing how much he should say, and then said. "It's a hobby. Some people buy expensive gold prospecting devices – cost a fortune they do. My rods are cheap and they work. It's a knack really. Some people have it and others don't. Like a lot of things I guess.""I've heard about it. My father told me they found water on our place down south using divining rods. Pump never failed while we lived there. Must be some truth to it, I guess."

He stepped back towards me and his eyes glowed with fire and enthusiasm."Geologists don't believe in them. Think I'm crazy. They'd rather believe in the black box bastards, those geo...geophysicists with their fancy cables and electrical stuff. Me, I like the rods. The ground talks to me and moves the rods. The geos can believe who they like, but I know the rods work. My way is cheaper and easier, and they do a fine job too. I can find water, they bloody well can't. Found gold in Canada with them when the geos had drilled sixty holes looking for it. I needed only one. They'd drilled in the wrong direction – common thing for geos to do. Gold I found was not economic though – veins too narrow for the company to mine it."

Embraced with enthusiasm as he saw that he had captured my attention, he continued."I can find faults. You know those big fractures in the ground – earthquakes cause them. I find buried wires, water pipes and water." He stopped remembering that he had told me about finding water."Amazing!""Not really, just a knack, a gift. Some people....," he stopped again as he recalled having explained it before.Clever chap I thought. "What are you looking for here?"

Then I remembered he had told me already. Must be the heat affecting us."How do they work...the rods I mean? How do you find minerals with them?" I quickly asked as he gave me an inquisitive look sensing I wanted to pick his brain."Copper 'n gold," he politely replied giving me a wink. "Must be the heat." He looked at me smiling. "Supposed to be a porphyry copper system here or that's what Mac Mining said in one of their reports before they gave up the ground. I bought the licence cheap during the last resource bust. When the copper price plummeted because the Chinese said they didn't want any more. Mac wants it back. I want to find the ore first. Make my fortune out of this then I can retire to the Sunshine Coast." He laughed."Found anything?"

He squinted, then shaking his head, said "No!"Disappointed I started turning back towards the car. When he saw my movement he added quickly. "Not around here. Up the track a bit I got some strong signals. Followed it over there," he said waving in the direction from where he had walked. "Must be a fault that's cut it off. Need to spend more time figuring it out."

He offered me the empty water bottle, saying "Got to be goin'. Thanks for the drink."

I took the bottle, asking "You never said how they worked."

He had just started to walk away, but looked over his shoulder, answering "Ever tried it. Divining I mean?""No.""Well, it's like this. I think I can trust you and you seem like a smart fellow, so I'll tell it to you." The bright sparkle in his eyes had returned and he eagerly began his explanation."We're not just animals you know. We're walking electric batteries, full of electricity. A current flows through us all the time. That's how the brain works, passing electrical signals to different parts of the body. When we get sick it means the current's not flowing right. Wires are short-circuited and the current can't flow. Healthy people have a couple of volts and low current flowing. Ever got a spark off someone?" He paused, looking intently for my reaction. Before I could answer he said, "I did. A good looking sheila she was too. Married unfortunately!" he laughed. "All that static electricity – gives a good spark doesn't it? Where does that come from, eh?"

Kicking a black rock with his worn brown steel capped boot he refocused on his explanation."These rods," he said, as he lifted them up, one in each hand, are like my antennae. They receive electromagnetic waves from the earth as I walk around. They pick up signals from ore minerals like copper and gold. The current that flows through my body charges the rods and the signals from minerals interfere with their stability and they move with the flow of electrical energy. If there's nothing in the ground then they stay straight, but when I pass an electrical anomaly they turn inwards and cross each other. I don't make the rods do it. They do it because of the natural electrical imbalances.""I see," I said, not really understanding the physics."Scientists don't really understand it either," he said reading my response accurately. "But it does work.""Can you show me?""There's nothing around here. See, the rods are out in front." He dropped the left arm holding one rod to his side, then the other rod started to turn in the direction he had indicated, back up the track. "Told you. See. This one's pointing up there where I told you there's something.""What happens when you find something?""The rods cross over.""Can I follow you?""Sure!"

We walked a few paces. He held the rods, one in each fist with the long part of the L-shape pointing straight out in front."What's your name?" I asked."Keith Barnes, but everyone calls me Curly 'cos of my hair."

We continued walking and every now and again he would drop the left hand to his side and follow the direction of the rod in his right fist. We had walked a good three hundred metres or so when the single rod he held in front started to swing to the right. "It's over this way," he said following the direction.

He held both rods in front and continued walking. Then he stopped. Standing behind him I couldn't see the rods."Look!" he said.I walked past him and observed the two wires crossed over each other. "This is where it starts."He dropped both rods to his side. "Stay there."

He walked back the way we had come, then turned to face me and held the rods in front. They were parallel to each other and the ground. As he walked towards me the rods swung until they crossed."I see.""Copper's probably here. Chalco's my bet.""What's chalco?""Chalcopyrite. It's one of the copper ores.""How do you know that?""It looks like this," he said, opening his right fist to show me a bright yellow lump of rock.

He closed the fist around the wire rod and continued walking. The rods were crossed as he walked at a steady pace across the flat towards a creek with a handful of tall, thin twisted white gums standing resolutely along the banks. He stopped when the rods uncrossed."Probably a fault here too, cuts it off. It's about seventy metres wide. Bigger than a vein. I've followed this signal for a kilometre now so I think I've got an ore body here.""How do you know that?""I pace it out. I find where the signal starts and then I follow it until the rods uncross. I figure out how wide and how long. If it's big enough I can estimate the size of the mine."

I thought a moment and then realized his error. "But," I began hesitatingly because of my lack of knowledge on the subject. "What if the ore is not vertical? How can you measure the angle or the depth?"

He swung around and smiled."Smart fellow! You're smarter than you look. Thing is we never know until it's drilled. Can't measure the dip or depth. Geos can measure the dip if it crops out, but we can't measure the depth.""Why not?""Just can't. If I could do that, then I'd be rich. Nice talking to you, but must head off. Trucks parked over there under those gums. Thanks again for the water. Have a good weekend. See ya!"

I walked back to my car that I'd left standing in the sun. It would be bloody hot inside. Have to park it in shade next time. One thing occupied my mind as I walked back, "How could he estimate the depth?"

Canadian Gold

Charlie Simpson is 72 years, a staunch Québecer, about 173cm (5'8") and has short dark straight hair, bifocals and a grinning face. To give you a clue about his sense of humour he tells a joke by asking a question. "Do you know why Jesus was not born in Quebec? They couldn't find a virgin or three wise men!" Then he follows up with a comment on Bruce's weak coffee:"It's like making love in a canoe: fucking close to water." He also describes a difficult time he was having nailing some wood. "It was like a dog fucking a football!"

On 16 January fifty years ago he married Caroline. She stands about 168cm with short blonde hair. Her roundish face perches on a small body and she is always on the go. She works the computer and corresponds with their three sons and one daughter using email. Charlie knows about computers but leaves the key strokes to Caroline.

Kevin is a geologist staying at the Charlton Lodge while supervising a gold drilling project in British Columbia and working with Charlie in his garage that they have converted into a core logging shed. Connie Daville and Bruce Tipping run the Charlton Lodge. Connie was married previously but is divorced - her previous husband died a few years ago. Bruce is slightly younger and has lived all his life in the region of the gold mines. He has seen the Pacific Ocean, once when he was a lad; his parents took him in winter one year; the Atlantic Ocean is just too far east for him to contemplate travelling there; he might go to Calgary one day. He has never been very far south except to fish in the lake three miles away. Bruce drives machinery for the County and used to drive snow ploughs in winter, but his eye sight is deteriorating; macular degeneration, so only works day shift. He smokes resulting in corroded teeth with gaps between brown stained residual prongs. His speech is affected by hesitation saying things like "I was telling her about, err- hum, what I meant to say, err- hum, I was telling her about, err-hum....I saw a moose carcass err-hum on the side of the road. Did you see it? Err-hum, it should not've been there as the season's over."

Bruce drives a front-end loader at the municipal rubbish tip. He complains that people drive in to dump their rubbish when he is about to go on a lunch or tea-break, forcing him, in his break to scoop their dumped rubbish and transport it to the desired heap. "No consideration," he says. "You'd think they would know to bring their trash in early in the morning, err-hum, not any old time of the day, err-hum particularly not around lunch!"

Bruce's wife, Connie must be in her late sixties. She is tall, wears glasses, has short straight grey hair cropped close. She's a talker with a great welcoming smile and penetrating gaze. She almost burnt the house down just after Kevin arrived. She had left a pan of fat on the hotplate and it caught fire. She wandered through the house carrying the hot blazing pot, panicking. Not knowing what to do she dropped the flaming pan in the sink and turned on the tap. Flames shot up to the ceiling causing blackening. Luckily, Kevin who was standing nearby grabbed a tea towel and ignoring the flames held it under the tap briefly before dropping it over the incendiary pot.

Bruce cooks breakfast and Connie makes dinner. The meals are basic English fare. Eggs cooked different ways and toast form Bruce's limited menu. The last two nights Connie cooked roast pork and roast chicken with coleslaw, mashed potatoes, and peas; nothing exotic or extravagant.

The country around the Lodge is a pine forest pock marked by swamps and highly prospective for gold. Several old mines exploited deep veins rich in gold, but then the vein formed a lens and the gold mining stopped. New companies came, drilled deeper boreholes and then left when they couldn't find any high grade mineralisation.

Another company has been successfully drilling a long way north and west of the town, and have been having better luck. They have found several potential mines and have drilling crews working around the clock proving up resources.

The ground in between those leases is held by a different company. They bought the ground from a businessman who wanted to sell out before he died. He did just that and now they are drilling again. Previous geologists had drilled to the north looking for high-grade gold, and they found some the year before. Now they are back looking to prove up a resource so they can either mine it or sell the lease for a profit.

Francis Holden, a young geologist had spent several days walking over the property to measure the trends and dip angles of faults and veins. She checked on the collar coordinates of previous drill holes. Back in her office she collated all the assay data from the previous sixty five drill holes, fitted it to a map and determined a strategy for the drill-out pattern. The high-grade gold intersections formed an approximate spindle-shaped pattern that pointed at a low angle to the southwest, or that's what she estimated, but it was a very approximate guess. The plan she developed was to drill three holes from each of three platforms located fifty metres apart on the western side of the hill. Each of the holes would be at a different angle, 45, 60 and 70 degrees below the horizontal and would intersect, or so she believed, the high-grade gold-bearing system at specified depths that she had roughly calculated. As a drilling crew were mobilising to the site the manager of the company, Tony Hatchet found himself in a predicament. He had endorsed the drilling program and strongly recommended to the Board of his company that they drill according to Holden's plan. It was just what the company needed to demonstrate an ore body and then they could sell the property and then the Board members, who owned most of the shares, would become rich. Hatchet's problem was that Francis Holden needed urgent hospital care and would not be able to supervise the drilling program. Where could Hatchet find another geologist quickly?

Fortunately, Hatchet had recently contacted his old Australian friend, Kevin, about another matter and he knew Kevin might take up the challenge of supervising the program at short notice. He phoned. Kevin was living near Santa Fe, New Mexico, and available. After negotiating a price for the work Hatchet relaxed, contacted the drilling company and confirmed the starting date, then asked his assistant to arrange travel, clothing and accommodation at the Lodge for Kevin.

Kevin flew to the site and met Charlie who showed him around the town and the mining lease, and the locations of the drilling platforms. The drillers arrived on time; friendly, safety conscious and efficient. All was going well. The accommodation was great. Kevin and Charlie formed an affable team with Charlie providing an all-terrain vehicle, a warm garage, tables to support the trays of drill core for Kevin to log and mark the core for cutting, powerful lighting so Kevin could study the core and a hydraulic splitter so that half of each core could be sent for assaying to determine its gold content.

At the Lodge, Connie and Bruce were great hosts. The drilling crew, from Quebec spoke English and French, and have years of experience. Their equipment is new and the orientation device to mark the bottom of the core for structural measurements works well. This would allow Kevin to measure the trend and dip of veins, particularly thin iron sulphide (pyrite) veins. Charlie had never seen this done before. He was very optimistic that this drilling program and new technique would find enough gold to mine.

Just when everything was working perfectly things turned sour. It was the start of winter; the temperature plummeted and snow fell in thick heavy clusters of flakes. Beaver dams they drove past to reach the rig froze over. Puddles developed thick ice layers that crunched when crossed by the all-terrain vehicle. Each morning Charlie lit a fire in his new stove to heat the garage so the core could thaw out before Kevin started looking at it.

On the morning after the third hole was drilled and Kevin had finished examining the core he knew he had a problem. "Like many things," Kevin began, a frustrating tone tinging his Australian accent as he caught Charlie's attention. "When everything seems like it is going well something changes and the arse falls out. Where in the hell is the gold deposit. I thought they were supposed to be drilling out a mine here!"

Charlie was a little slow to grasp the sudden outburst because he was busy stoking the fire and struggling with a piece of birch that was too big to fit in the stove. He is also slightly deaf and because of his pre-occupation with the cantankerous piece of wood that he fought to place precisely in the fire Charlie did not hear Kevin's frustrated outburst.

"Fucking gold mine. I thought Hatchet said I was here to prove the resource. I want to know where the hell the gold is," Kevin continued agitatedly.

Charlie looked up and said, "You talking to me?"

"No. I'm swearing at frigging Hatchet. I thought they were drilling out a gold mine. The program was simple. Drill nine holes and calculate a resource. You seen any bloody gold? I haven't."

"No."

"Well, where the hell is it? Three flaming holes and nothing. Just some pyrite veins and a little sniff of chalco, copper. All I've been doing is measuring pyrite veins and the structure tells me the mineralisation is not where they think it is."

"Where is it then?"

"All I know is it is not where the plan said it was going to be. We need to change the program. Got Hatchet's number? I'll call the bastard."

"Just a minute. I have his number here somewhere," Charlie said rummaging through scraps of paper on the bench and old torn pieces of cardboard pinned by nails to the garage wall. He found the number written in pencil on a white post above the telephone. Dialling he connected to the party line of the house phone and heard his wife, Caroline talking to her sister. "Excuse me love, we need to call Hatchet urgently," Charlie said calmly. "Can you talk a little later?"

He smiled, covered the mouth piece with his hand saying, "She's gossiping to her sister. They meet every other day to go shopping, yet they still talk each day."

Charlie listened, then dialled the number when the line was available. When Hatchet answered, they exchanged greetings politely and talked about the weather outside Hatchet's office window in Toronto, the weather at the garage, how their wives were feeling, an outstanding payment for equipment hire and his impending visit. Charlie broke the conviviality by interrupting

Hatchet."Kev wants a word. See you tomorrow night then. I've booked you and the missus in at the Lodge."

Kevin exchanged pleasantries and learnt again of Hatchet's imminent visit, and then told him about the lack of gold in the core. Hatchet was mystified and did not have a reasonable answer. He fobbed Kevin off by saying that he will arrive tomorrow and will discuss it then.

Disgruntled, Kevin hung up the phone, shrugged his shoulders and looking at Charlie said, "he's got no frigging clue."

"Well, that's three in a boat," Charlie replied. "No oar, no fish and a gaping hole. We need it to freeze fast so the boat doesn't sink. We could walk out then! Like my bleeding fire, cold as a pork chop at a Jewish picnic!"

Charlie attended to his fire while Kevin went about his business of marking the core, measuring structural features and writing rock descriptions on his log sheets. After a while they stopped for morning tea, their usual practice.

Charlie arranged two old armchairs in the corner of his garage, near the fire, but not too close that they would overheat when they sat down for a break. Caroline usually made a thermos of tea and packed sandwiches, cakes and two mars bars each. Charlie handed his Mars bars over to Kevin; not too good for his triple by pass."'bout time you stopped," Charlie said grinning slyly at Kevin as he took the lid off the thermos that Connie had made.

"I ate early," he continued. "Got up at 5.30 and made the wife a cuppa tea, then ate breakfast. It's 10.30 and I'm starving. It's all right for you young fellows who get up late."

Kevin took the bait and bit back, "I was working on this bloody gold shit since 5 myself. Had to wait 'til 6.30 to get Bruce's breakfast. Dozy bastard forgot to make coffee again."

Charlie grinned. "Good old reliable Bruce!"

"At least Connie's on the boil. She's a great cook. Don't know how she puts up with him."

"Not too many choices round here you know. I got the best one. Caroline's from Rouyn Noranda. Connie had to take the lean pick'ns available and Bruce just happened to be it."

"So, Hatchet's coming tomorrow. What's he gonna say? Nothing! He knows nothing. Thinks he knows where the ore body is cos he's got this idea gold forms in saddle reefs and there is one here that, what's his name, the other geo found."

"Tomkinson. Hugh Tomkinson drilled here last year. Last hole they hit lots of VG. Saw the visible gold myself. Hatchet was thrilled."

"Well we haven't seen any bloody visible gold in three drill holes. You've looked and you can't see it. I've looked with my hand lens at every bloody metre of core and can't see a trace of it. Can't even see any alteration either. How in the hell someone can say the gold mineralisation has a certain shape and size and predicts where it is, and then when you drill the designated target there's no bloody sign of it. You sure you saw VG last year. You weren't pissed were you?"

Charlie listened respectfully to his ramblings, then asked, "Who planned the program?"

"That sheila from Sudbury. She was convinced she knew where the gold was."

"I showed her around for a few days. Seemed nice. Young though!"

"Well she flaming well got it wrong. You have to admit it."

Charlie changed the subject and talked about his son and his family, and how Hatchet owed him money. He talked about other prospects, anything to distract Kevin. He finished by talking about busting a beaver dam. Charlie disliked beavers.

When Hatchet arrived late the following day, Charlie and Kevin had laid out a full table of core, and then added another layer of core trays over the top of those. Kevin's frustration had grown throughout the day because the core drilled the previous night also did not have any visible gold in it.

Hatchet expressed amazement by what he saw, barren core. Charlie and Kevin lifted pieces of core, washed them in warm water from a bucket standing near the fire and examined them under a magnifying lens. They showed Hatchet. Nothing! No visible gold.

All Hatchet could say was "Amazing. Hugh drilled lots of gold last year. You remember seeing it Charlie. You've got it wrong, Kevin. You have to drill in the same direction as Hugh. You're not doing it right."

Kevin stared at Hatchet. What could he say? He was following a program worked out by someone else, and the plan had been totally endorsed by Hatchet. Now, Kevin's so called mate was blaming him for not finding the gold. Charlie interrupted the train of thought by telling Hatchet about the orientation marks.

"No one else did what Kev's been doing. No one understands the rocks better than he does. He makes all these measurements and figures out angles and stuff, then tries to figure it out on paper. He will find the gold if anyone can."

Hatchet looked absently at Charlie, as if ignoring what he had said."Hugh knows where it is," Hatchet replied.

Kevin's disgust abated so he asked Hatchet, "Got any historical drilling reports I can read?"

"Hugh's sent them to the office. I'll get my assistant to send them up to you. There's about six years worth of drilling data. Could be useful."

"Anybody collate the material? Make a composite map or section drawings?" Kevin asked.

Hatchet's blank expression revealed to Kevin Hatchet knew nothing about any previous analytical work. "Hugh knows," Hatchet said dismissively, turning to walk out of the garage.

When Hatchet had driven off from the garage Kevin let out a tirade of abuse. The essence of which was that Hatchet was a flaming idiot who knew nothing. His final remark before suggesting to Charlie that they drink a beer was that "if fucking Hugh knew where the gold was then why in fucking hell wasn't he here drilling it out?"

They sat silently drinking the beers Charlie had taken from his fridge. "You'll break my bank the way you drink my beer," Charlie said, looking sideways at Kevin.

"I'll buy you some beer the next time we go to town."

"I was just joking. I get it cheaper in Alberta than in BC. It's nothing. Hear the one about the Irishman, the Canadian and the Australian?"

Charlie related his joke to laughter and told several more as they drank their beers. After a few more empty beer bottles piled up on the floor Kevin thought it was time he headed back to the lodge for supper.

Three days later two large cardboard boxes arrived with the historic drilling reports Kevin had asked Hatchet to provide. Kevin spent the next few nights studying the reports, plotting maps and compiling the data. Meanwhile each drilling shift resulted in 30m or more of core Kevin had to examine for gold, but still there was no trace of the high-grade; a few thin chalcopyrite veins and more pyrite, but no VG.

Hatchet phoned each day complaining that Kevin did not know what he was doing. He kept repeating. " there is no gold because you are drilling in the wrong place. Only Hugh knows where it is." One morning, Hatchet called and told Kevin he must call Hugh because he knows where the gold is. He could tell Kevin where to drill next.

Kevin's response was expected, "If that bastard knew where the gold was then why in the hell wasn't he here drilling? Why hadn't Hatchet asked Hugh to supervise the program and not me?"

"You gonna call Hugh?" Charlie asked.

"No. Fuck him!"

"Didn't Hatchet say he had called Hugh and for him to expect your call," Charlie enquired. "You'd better call because Hatchet will call Hugh and find out you never called him. Then you will be in deep shit."

Kevin picked up another piece of core and half-heartedly studied it, his mind sorting out what to do. He looked at several more pieces while considering his options. Putting the last piece of core back in its place in the core tray Kevin reluctantly asked Charlie for Hugh's number.

As Charlie had met Hugh last year and worked with him he made the call and chatted. He found out that Hugh was expecting to hear from Kevin because Hatchet had called him several times explaining the problem. Kevin took the phone from Charlie and explained the situation briefly. They discussed the issue for a few minutes before Kevin asked, "Where should I drill next?"

"I don't know," Hugh replied before following up with a suggestion. "Ernie Galloway drilled a shallow hole in 2006 that hit high grade gold. You should drill where he did. It was hole 6-12 and hit gold at 17m."

"OK. Can you tell me why most people drilled from the southeast to the northwest or back the other way from what's in the current plan?"

"Just the structure. It looks like the trend is northeast."

"Thanks."

"Any time you need advice give me a call," Hugh offered. "Hatchet says I'm to help as much as I can. Would like to be up there myself but have other rigs operating that I need to supervise."

Kevin hung up the phone, looked at Charlie and after laughing said, "Fucking idiots! Hatchet and Hugh know fuck all. Drill another hole alongside a Galloway hole chasing the high-grade he found. What an arsehole! All Hatchet wants is a great intersection so he can write a flaming good news release. Hole 6-12 is in basalt and it's got nothing to do with the chalcopyrite-gold mineralisation in the diorite that I'm supposed to be proving a resource in. The gold in the basalt relates to black-smokers – it's volcanogenic. The gold in the diorite is a hydrothermal vein: two distinct environments. You can see that in the old reports. There's a flaming great fault between the two zones."

"What're you going to do?"

"Figure it out. The only thing I've got is the structural data I've measured from the last few holes and a rough idea where they intersected the high-grade in the past,....and a fucking old tart for an assistant."

"Now don't get like that. I may be old, but I'm not a tart and I don't fuck any more. No lead in the old pencil!"

"No one to write to! Ha!"

Both erupted in laughter. "Let's have an early lunch."

Just after they sat and began to eat and drink tea the phone rang. Charlie answered, then said, "the old woman." His wife transferred the call. "Hatchet wants a word," Charlie said, a smile spreading cheekily across his face.

"Shit! Not again."

Kevin stood and took the phone from Charlie who had started chuckling to himself much to Kevin's annoyance. Hatchet talked to Kevin who sharply kicked at the leg of the bench with his steel capped boot. Kevin scribbled a few notes on a sheet of paper and then hung up.

"What did he want?" Charlie asked as Kevin returned to his chair by the fire.

"Wanted to know whether I spoke with Hugh. I explained what Hugh and I discussed then Hatchet told me to find the high-grade by drilling as Hugh had done. Drill another hole alongside the one in which Hugh had found high-grade."

"So now you have two holes to drill; the Galloway hole and a twin of Hugh's."

"Not fucking likely," Kevin fumed.

Charlie looked blankly at Kevin and to give him time to think he took a bite into a pickle, cheese and salami sandwich. Kevin poured another mug of tea. They sat silently eating and drinking.

"I need to take more measurements and plot up the data. Hatchet was going to buy a software package called Leapfrog to help with the structural interpretation, but it's too expensive."

"What's Leapfrog? I thought it was a kid's game."

"It's a computer program the structural guys use to interpret their data. All those measurements I'm making go into a spreadsheet and then the program displays the orientations of veins and joints. It helps the geologist see what the structure is doing and where mineralisation might be localised. Cheapskate! I'll plot the data by hand. It looks like there's a trend running to the southeast and dipping northeast, but I need more measurements. If it is running southeast then all the previous holes we've been drilling have been almost parallel to that trend. No wonder we haven't hit any VG, we're drilling parallel to the structure, not across it. Historically, when they drilled from the south they drilled down the structure, but then occasionally a hole deviated off direction near its end and it turned across the mineralisation giving a false impression of location and thickness of the VG. Hatchet and Hugh have no idea what's really going on. Hatchet just wants me to do the same to get a good high-grade intersection so he can report it to the stock exchange."

"I knew those measurements would be useful. No one has done that before. I'm sure it'll tell us where the gold is," Charlie responded grinning.

After lunch, they went back to work. Charlie noisily split the core in halves, placed one half in a calico bag and the other back in the tray. He followed the sheet of depth intervals Kevin had given him. The samples in the bags would be sent for gold and copper analyses. Kevin wanted to make sure they had not missed any VG, so after Charlie had split the core they both examined the broken pieces; still no gold.

Kevin took structural measurements by reassembling long lengths of core. He marked the bottom of the core with a black permanent marker. With the selected pieces of core he propped them in a wooden frame Charlie had made to make it easier to measure the dip and strike of veins. The frame held a V-notched piece of wood angled at the dip of the drill hole. The frame and core were turned so they faced both the dip and the direction the hole was drilled. The orientation is called the azimuth. Kevin measured dip and strike angles of the mineral veins and wrote them in his notebook. Each night he plotted the angles using pencil and paper to see the orientations of the mineralised vein structures to illustrate the geometry of the gold mineralisation.

Each day passed with frequent calls from Hatchet. Kevin refused to drill as instructed, but had picked two locations where he thought he could obtain useful structural data and possibly also intersect gold. He had minor success finding several thin veins containing chalcopyrite. He thought he was close to finding the gold deposit. Charlie answered Hatchet's calls and occasionally informed him about Kevin, saying he was at the rig, when Kevin was standing in the garage a few metres away. Whenever the phone rang Kevin instructed Charlie, "If that's fuckin' Hatchet, tell him I'm at the rig. I don't want to talk to the bastard."

One day Charlie couldn't lie anymore and handed the phone to Kevin who reluctantly took it, poking a threatening fist at Charlie who chuckled as he walked away. The message Hatchet had for Kevin was clear, "Drill a hole the same as Hugh's high-grade intersection."

Charlie heard Kevin agree, but then when Kevin hung up the phone Kevin said to him, "Not on your bloody life. I'll collar it where he wants me to, but I'll change the angle and drill across what I think is the strike and not along it."

"That'll cause trouble!"

"What the hell. We are no closer than when we started. Nobody knows where the hell the gold is. How am I to find it if I follow what everyone else has done? They got lucky. I'm sure the answer is in understanding the structure."

"Did I tell you the one about the holes in the snow and why there are two sorts? There are round holes with a single trailing line from each and then there are a series of narrow slits. Bet you can't guess why that's so?"

Kevin thought for a minute considering various wild animals he knew, but couldn't think of an answer.

Charlie beamed. "Men create the first sort 'cos they stand in one place. The other sort are created by women who can't squat still for long, but have to keep moving to see who's about," Charlie retorted, laughing while adding another piece of core to the splitter. Crunch!

The next day, after the drillers had brought the core into the garage and Kevin had briefly inspected it he told Charlie to look at a specific piece containing a bright yellow metallic band about 1cm wide.

"What do you think of that?"

"Looks like a vein of chalcopyrite."

"Right, but look where it is," Kevin said, his eyes shining enthusiastically. "It's running down the length of the core for about a metre. We're drilling down the flaming ore vein. Then it pinches out and starts again down here. Look!"

Charlie bent forward to look. "You're right. So what?"

"You silly old faggot, it means we're drilling down and not across the mineralisation. Just as I bloody well thought. This drill hole proves what I've suspected all along."

"That good?"

"Good and bad. Good because we've hit the mineralised vein and bad because it's in the wrong direction."

"Going to tell Hatchet?"

"Sure," Kevin said with a gleam in his eyes.

Charlie called Hatchet to tell him the good news and handed the phone to Kevin who happily reported the great news.

"You can't drill down a vein," Hatchet yelled, "It's not possible."

"We have! You can see the vein in the core."

"It's impossible,' Hatchet insisted. "You must have drilled across the vein. You can't drill down a vein."

"I tell you we are drilling in the wrong direction. We have to drill from the other side, back to the southwest."

"That's rubbish. Hugh and Galloway found the gold by drilling to the northwest and that's what I want you to do. Drill another hole parallel to Hugh's. Got that?"

"Sure." Kevin said before hanging up the phone.

"Fucking arsehole. He can't get it in his head that we have drilled down the vein. You can see it. It's not a fuckin' illusion."

"What does he want you to do?"

"Drill alongside Hugh's bonanza hole."

"Goin' to?"

"Nope."

Christmas was rapidly approaching and funds for the drilling program were shrinking, so Kevin had to make a decision. The drillers wanted to go home. They had been working for six weeks without a break and were tiring. The cold weather and snow did not help matters. Freezing water pipes in the night stopped the drilling until they laid out another pipe and heated the water before pumping it to the drill site.

Kevin surprised Charlie one morning by saying, "One last hole, Charlie you old bastard and then we'll call it quits. I've calculated where to drill to hit three veins of high-grade gold. Hatchet was onto me last night insisting I find the gold and give him something to report. The Board have been hounding him for good news. He's under the pump, poor bastard."

"Where are you going to drill?"

"I'll show you. I've done the calculations and the first two intersections should be easy, but the third is more difficult because it's a long way to extrapolate using the rough data from the other holes," Kevin explained smiling. "We will drill from the northeast to the southwest. Want to come out to shift the rig?"

"Sure, mate!"

They donned their warm clothing as the temperature was sub-zero and the chilling wind was blowing sharply from the north. Kevin started driving the hired all-terrain vehicle down the icy slope towards Charlie's house and onto the street, but in the freezing conditions the accelerator stuck at full throttle catapulting them down the hill. Kevin swore while turning the wheel to steer away from colliding with the house and Charlie, reacting quickly, reached across and turned the key to switch the engine off. The pair came to an abrupt stop a few metres from the wall of Charlie's house.

"That was fucking close," Kevin said looking at a startled Charlie. "Second time that's happened to me," Kevin explained. "Scares the shit out of me."

"Me too! Accelerator sticks. That's too dangerous. We'll take mine instead," Charlie offered

Kevin reversed the vehicle and once again Charlie's swift action prevented another accident as the accelerator stuck at full throttle.

"Leave the bastard there. I'm not driving it again," Kevin told Charlie who had already stepped out and was heading for his other garage. Charlie reversed his all-terrain vehicle outside and Kevin climbed in. They drove through icy puddles, deep snow drifts and along a track used by snowmobiles where the snow had been packed down. They easily crossed a previously treacherous stretch of boggy track because it was frozen solid. They arrived at the rig just as the offsider laid the last rod on the rack for a change of bit. Kevin examined the core before he told the driller they would move site. He found the bulldozer driver and instructed him to clear a track and pad at the new drill site Kevin identified using orange tape.

The drillers moved the rig after Donnie, the dozer driver had pushed over two large dead widow-maker trees and cleared scrub so the drilling shack could sit on level ground. Glenn, the driller used a chain saw to cut a large birch tree, selecting large blocks of the trunk to form a foundation for the shack so that it didn't sink into the mud. Kevin directed Donnie to push the shack with the bulldozer to align it in the direction he wanted the last hole drilled. Once Kevin had checked the angle of the rig to ensure it was at 60 degrees Charlie and Kevin drove back to the garage and let the drillers begin coring.

The next morning Kevin anxiously paced in the warm garage for the night-shift crew to bring the core. The drillers were late and Kevin worried whether there was a problem at the rig. Charlie stoked the fire and warmed a bucket of water so they could wash the cold core. Kevin shuffled edgily near the fire and fidgeted with tools strewn across Charlie's work bench, a grim look on his face. Charlie tried cracking a few jokes to relieve the tension, but Kevin was preoccupied thinking about the core. His professional reputation balanced precariously on the success of this drill hole. All his planning depended on the many structural measurements he had made and if he were wrong, then the drilling campaign would not only end on a sour note, but he would personally feel devastated because he had failed.

"Fuck this. I'm going out to the rig," Kevin shouted impatiently to Charlie.

"Patience boy-oh, patience," Charlie replied.

A sound at the door raised Kevin's excitement, expecting the drillers with the core trays, but seeing Caroline with their lunch shattered his enthusiasm. Eventually they heard the sound of a truck. Charlie raised the garage door so they could carry the core directly onto the bench they had already cleared in anticipation.

Each core tray was covered with a wooden lid taped at each end to prevent the core from rolling about. They carried in ten boxes, 30m of core from the night shift. Donnie explained that they were late because their all-terrain vehicle that they usually used to carry the core from the rig to the truck ran out of fuel. He had to walk to his truck and back to get a container so they could refuel it.

Charlie closed the garage door. Kevin took one of Charlie's fishing knives and cut the plastic wrapping around each of the core trays. Charlie used a chisel at the other end to remove the tape. They lifted the lids from the boxes and stacked them in the far corner of the garage. The temperature of the core was below freezing and the water they wiped on it to clean the surface froze instantly.

"We'll have to wait until it warms up," Charlie said as he returned to the fire to add more wood.

Kevin paced impatiently around the core trays, bending over now and then to peer at the cloudy frozen surface.

"Coffee?" Charlie offered.

Kevin walked over and sat with Charlie by the fire while they waited for the core to warm up.

"You'd better be right," Charlie said.

"I don't need you to tell me that. Hatchet will tell me soon enough that I've stuffed up and didn't do what he wanted me to do."

"I'm sure you're right," Charlie stated confidently. "All those measurements. No one has ever done that before. You understand the geology of this place better than anyone else. It will be fine, you'll see."

After about thirty minutes, Kevin went to look at the core. He checked his notebook for the depths he estimated the gold veins would be. "According to me the first mineralised vein should be at 68m. Bugger! They haven't reached that depth yet," Kevin said with disgust. "I'll go to the rig later and check."

"You said there were three intervals of gold. What are they?" Charlie quizzed."Sixty-eight, seventy-eight and 100m, why?"

"I want to know how smart you really are, Aussie. No one knows the rocks like you. We'll see how right you are when we check the intersections."

Kevin spent a frustrating morning logging the core and taking more measurements. Kevin was anxious to visit the rig to check on their progress and whether they had drilled through one of his postulated intervals. Charlie offered to drive Kevin after lunch. Kevin scratched around, swore unusually over minor frustrations, spilled his coffee, temporarily lost his compass and was generally like an anxious father waiting for the birth of his first child.

Finally, Charlie said the magic words, "Let's go."

Kevin slipped on his warm jacket and hat in a flash and was standing alongside the all-terrain vehicle before Charlie had a chance to add another log on the fire. They travelled in silence through the icy wind to reach the rig.

At the drilling site Kevin saw the boxes containing the core they had recently brought to the surface. The trays had caps already fitted and taped for transporting back to the truck. Kevin keenly took a scriber pen from his jacket and punctured the plastic bindings on a tray with the label 65-68m. Opening the lid Kevin gazed at the round cylindrical sticks of rock. "Fuck! Fuck! Fuck!" Kevin shouted, standing back, hands on hips.

Charlie opened the next box, 68-71m with his penknife. Kevin watched, dejected. The lid lifted off easily. Charlie looked at the core and pointing said, "Chalco! There's a vein a chalcopyrite."

Kevin's interest ignited. "Where! What depth?" He said bending down to look. "About sixty-eight and a half metres."

"You sure? Got a tape?"

Charlie handed Kevin a 3m tape measure and they ran it across the core measuring the depth from the labelled wooden core block.

"Sixty-eight forty-five! Fuckin' beauty. Not bad for a bloody Aussie eh, mate? Only out by 45 centimetres."

Charlie's smiling face said it all.

"Let's go back to the garage and a have a beer," Kevin said, slapping Charlie on his back.

"Bit early for that."

"Not too early to celebrate, mate. We've finally hit the gold target. Now for the other two intervals and we've pulled off a miracle."

The next day Kevin celebrated by drinking more of Charlie's beer. They measured two more intervals of gold-bearing sulphide at 85.2m and 105.07m.

"Not bad at extrapolating," Kevin told Charlie. "Out by 45 centimetres, seven metres and five metres, but we hit the three gold-bearing chalcopyrite veins. Pretty damn good for a flaming Aussie, eh?"

"You'll have to wait til the assays come back to be sure," Charlie cautioned.

"I'm right, I'm always fucking right. Don't you worry about that, as Jo Petersen used to say. We found it Charlie and that's all that counts. Now I can tell Hatchet exactly where he can stick his gold."

Indeed, a week later when Charlie phoned the assay results through to Kevin they had found more than 2, 15 and 3 gms/tonne gold in the three mineralised intervals, just as Kevin had predicted.

Hatchet wasn't pleased because they had not found 45gms/tonne or more as he expected. Consequently he refused to pay Kevin for the report he wrote detailing all the drill hole information, the structural measurements and the assay results. Years later Kevin is still waiting for Hatchet to pay him, because as far as Hatchet is concerned Kevin never did find the high-grade gold.

The Gull

The gull hung motionlessly, effortlessly, like an image in a landscape painting of a cliff and pounding ocean. White foamy spray splashed skywards below, far below the bird. And then the bird glided to one side without ruffling any feathers as if on a string being pulled by some invisible force. The string pulled again and gracefully the gull streamed along the cliff edge, seeking other vistas. A pair of staring eyes watched it wheel away, peeling off in the wind. In the mood he was in he imagined doing the same.

Simply take the step into the air and hover like the gull, he said to himself. Easy or so he felt, and in one action he too could sense the rush of air, allowing the force of nature to carry him away. What held him back?

He looked far out to sea at the line between air and ocean, and saw a parallel in his life; a boundary clear and sharp, like life and death. His life and his death with a sharp line in between. So easy for an artist to draw yet hard, impossibly hard for him to cross the line, and yet he had to make the mark. He had to draw his line; his line in his life, but how?

His friends sat nearby enjoying the view oblivious to his plight. They knew not what he thought and would have said so later if he had emulated the bird. They would have expressed utter surprise for he had hidden every thought. Their reactions would not be his concern because he would have drawn his line, and he would be happy he had done it. Or would he? Perhaps he could have drawn another line, less sharp, more blurred, but how?

Answers never seemed to come to him unless he fell into a bottomless pit, a chasm, an abyss, and then just as it seemed as though he would hit the deepest point a light would flicker and change everything. Well, sometimes it worked that way. He had been there before and knew the pattern well. The hardest part was falling, not knowing when the crunch will come and end it all. That is why by flying like a bird he would be safe. He could escape the problems in his head and soar, just glide along the cliff of life balanced by the wind. No effort really, just step onto the ledge of air and waft gently on its current to float along in blissful peace. Now, there's nothing wrong with that; easy. Just do it.

His head spun with thoughts and emotions choked his body. Like the rock he stood on he was fixed to the earth and could not budge. Too much, too many thoughts cascaded in his head, and yet the simple thought of flying eased all his tensions and gave relief. He could do it, he knew. He would be the first to fly without wings. Wings are not necessary. Just step out and the upward rushing air will carry you with it along the cliff face like the bird, he contemplated.

Why fly now, he thought. There are other things to do and say, and write and learn. But what is the point, when all alone he saw the world and everything in it was a black empty spot. The colourless spot held nothing. It was an empty shape without texture and meaning. It was just a spot, a black depressing hole, like the pit he had known before. So flying was the answer, but how?

How to solve the puzzle, the riddle and the complexities of life was by flying like a bird. It all made sense. Just step onto the blanket of air and float away. Do it now!

Facing the real problem was the challenge, not flying. Flying was easy. The real challenge was to find the reason for his stupidity. Why did he marry someone he never loved? Why did he do that twice? Only an idiot would do such things and not learn from their mistakes. Not him, because he is intelligent and clever, imaginative and creative. Or that is what everyone said. Not him, because his ego would not let him fail. He never failed, did he? Yes, there were exams he had failed, but they were nothing in comparison to this. Those tests were foolish things because the teachers knew the answers. Why ask such stupid questions when the real questions were out there unanswered; the cause of cancer, a cure for aids, and other new scientific discoveries to be made. That is what they should be asking. What does cause cancer? Then once the answer to that question is known find out the cure, but how?

By not giving up your life, you idiot. That's how!Did somebody speak over his shoulder? He turned, but nobody was standing there.

Not by flying like the bird, but by wiping the slate clean in a different way and starting from a new beginning. End one life and start another. It is how it can be done, the voice said. It is how it can be done, the voice repeated. Was it the sun peaking a glimpse through a dark cloud overhead or was it the solution to his problem he had been searching for? He did not know, but what he felt was a sudden urge to move. The bright light flickered in his eyes. Where was the gull? To back away from the edge so he could follow the thought some more, and pursue it to its end.

And then a plan began to form from the idea. His eyes squinted against the setting sun. If he were brave enough to take the pain then he could begin again and set out on another course. People would be hurt, and he amongst them too, but the outcome would be best for all and give him a chance to flourish. He decided after all he did not want to fly, but keep firmly on the ground. It rooted him to a sound foundation and from it he could metamorphose.

Rejoining his friends he smiled and seemed refreshed, or so they said. Inspired, he thought; a chance to go onto better things. The black spot had vanished like the bird, but would it stay away or haunt him yet again? At least for now some colour had returned and a distant goal seemed possible, a fringe of green on the golden orb marking the horizon.

Coffee on the Moon

The waiter brought four cups to the table in the Hindley Street cafe and set them down. Molly thanked him then asked his name.

"Thomas, but call me Tom," he said as he served Jonas, one of Molly's friends, sitting next to her. Bruce and Keith sat opposite. Bruce kept talking as Tom laid a cappuccino on the table in front of him, carefully avoiding Bruce's swirling hand gestures,

"Because there is no gravitational pull on the moon," Bruce explained. "It will neither fall towards the moon because there is no gravity to pull it there nor is there any other gravitational force that will pull it away from the moon. The Earth's too far away."

"But there is gravity!" Keith said emphatically, "and when you let the cup go it would fall."

"Yeah!" Jonas agreed as he reached for a paper satchel of brown sugar.

"Who says?" Bruce asked.

"Einstein!" Keith said

"Newton!" Molly corrected.

"Bullshit! There isn't any gravity," Jonas explained.

"Einstein did science stuff. He knew," Keith qualified as he spooned the froth from his cup.

"Well, of sorts. He worked on light not stars and space, and stuff, like astrologists do," Jonas said as Tom served the remaining coffees.

"You guys. It's not astrology you fools, it's astronomy," Molly corrected. "You're hopeless. It was Newton, Sir Isaac Newton."

"Where does he hang out?" Bruce asked with a grin before sipping his coffee. "Hey Tom, can you bring some milk."

"Isaac Newton came up with a formula to explain gravity," Molly hastily added.

"Yeah!" Jonas agreed. "E equals em and sea squared. I'm positive that's it."

"Really! How'd you know that?" Bruce asked just as Molly was about to say something, but closed her mouth when Keith quickly added "E equals mc squared, but that was Einstein who said it. Where does gravity come into it?"

"I don't understand how a doctor could be so smart and know all about astronomy. He's a doctor and not a scientist," Jonas said.

"What are you on about? He was a physicist! And Newton's dead," Molly said as her companions sipped their drinks. Tom brought a small nickel-plated jug of milk.

"Is it hot?" Molly asked.

"Warm," Tom replied. "Can I get you anything else?"

"No, I think we're right now. Thanks!" Molly said.

Keith nodded as Jonas concentrated on his thoughts, scratched his head and asked, "Tell me this then. If you dropped your cup here now and there was no gravity what would happen?"

"It'd spill the coffee and the cup'd smash," Bruce said.

"Nar! It would float about," Keith replied waving his hands like a magician conjuring a card trick.

"The formula's wrong," Molly said. "Let's fix that first before getting onto hypothetical questions."

"How come you know it's wrong?" Jonas interjected before she could explain. "Think you're smarter than us?"

"Well, she doesn't have the looks, so she must be smart," Bruce said grinning. Molly gave him a dirty look, and made a mental note to get even with him for that comment in the future.

Molly shuffled on her seat before saying, "it's f equals m times g, you clowns."

"What is?" Jonas asked.

"The bloody formula," Keith said slapping his arm with the back of his hand. "Aren't you paying attention?"

"Nope, I was figuring out the coffee cup floating off into the air," Jonas sighed thoughtfully.

"There wouldn't be any air if there was no gravity, dumb wit!" Bruce said.

"How come?" Keith and Jonas asked simultaneously.

"Gravity keeps the air on the Earth. No gravity, then no air."
Molly said. "So you'd die. Bugger the coffee cup, you'd be dead."

"So the cup would float off if he dropped it then," Jonas posed.

"No, it would stay where it was. No gravity and it would hang,"
Molly suggested.

"Hang on what? Tell me that? You're real smart Moll, but you're
wrong. Be like the air and float off into space," Bruce explained
positively.

"But we were talking about a coffee on the Moon, and not here.
So what would happen there?"

"Dropped your coffee there, you mean?" Bruce queried.

"Yeah. Like, if we was all sitting in a coffee shop on the Moon
for instance, and you dropped your coffee what would happen?
Would it float, cup and coffee fall to the surface or the cup be
pulled to Earth?" Keith asked.

"It would…." Molly started to say, but Jonas interrupted.

"I think it would….Now Molly, give me a chance to go first. You
always butt in and say stuff that confuses us, so let me go first ok?
I'll tell you what would happen."

"Ok. Tell us what would happen, Jonas."

"It would float where it is and not move because there is no
gravitational pull. It will not float away unless it is pushed. The
gravity on the moon won't pull it to the surface, and since the cup

won't make any movement on its own, it should float where it is. There's got to be a force acting on it before it moves. There is no gravity, so the coffee stays in the cup," Jonas said assertively.

"First of all," Keith said, "the coffee would spill out as there is nothing to keep it in the cup. It would sink to the ground slowly and the cup would fall to the surface first, it's heavier."

"You're wrong!" Bruce exclaimed. Don't you know that the gravity of the Earth is stronger than on the Moon, so the pull from the Earth would drag the cup and coffee together to Earth."

"Never thought of that," Jonas said. "You're right. That makes sense."

"Theoretically," Bruce said as he sat back and rubbed his chin authoritatively, as if he was a lecturer about to give an important presentation. "It should float away because it has no mass. Gravity does not pull the cup towards the surface at a rate great enough to make it fall, however it does have enough force to keep it floating, but ultimately it will drift away."

"Where to? Where's the force come from? Where would it go? Earth?" Jonas asked keen to find an ally for his argument.

"Just into space," Bruce added.

"But the gravitational force on the Moon is about one sixth of the Earth," Molly advised.

"So the cup of coffee will float away towards the Earth because the gravitational pull of the moon is less," Jonas said encouragingly, "so I'm right."

"No," Bruce stated pushing his empty cup away, "if the gravitational pull on the Moon is approximately one sixth of the Earth's, then it will not be enough to cause the cup to fall nor remain stationary. The gravitational pull of other objects would influence the cup, so it would float to the strongest gravity object."

"And that's the Earth," Jonas insisted, butting in.

"Look, you guys," Molly began agitatedly, "the cup would fall to the Moon's surface and you'd be toast because there's no atmosphere. Get it?"

"Ignore her," Jonas said, "she doesn't know what she's talking about. The gravity is so low and there's no atmosphere, no wind or anything, so it just floats away depending which way you push it."

Bruce and Keith nodded their heads in agreement. Molly shook her head to disagree and asked, "Well, tell me this. What would happen if one day gravity stopped on Earth and we were here drinking coffee and you dropped a cup? Let's make it an empty cup for simplicity. What would happen? Would it fall like today when there is gravity, or float like you guys say it will on the Moon?"

"That's easy," Jonas said. "It would float and be pulled by the Moon because the Moon's got gravity, weak, but it's still got it. The cup would head to the Moon, slow like, but it would go there. If there was coffee in the cup it would run out and fall to the ground."

Keith and Bruce looked at each other, then at Jonas. Molly sat silently with a bemused look on her face.

"I get the cup floating off Jonas, but I don't see why the coffee would run to the ground," Keith queried.

"Simple," Jonas explained. "Coffee's a liquid and it runs. The cup's heavy and because it's heavier it would be pulled by the Moon's gravity and tip the cup so the coffee would run out. Molly here, is the smart one, and says the Moon's got gravity. She says the formula, f equals m times g proves it. M is the mass and g is gravity. That's right Moll, isn't it?"

He waited for Molly's agreeing nod before continuing. "So the mass of the cup and the Moon's gravity means that the cup is pulled that way; to the moon. The coffee is lighter and runs to Earth. It's a liquid, not a solid."

Molly almost choked on her last sip of coffee.

"You alright Moll," Keith asked.

"Yeah! Just went down the wrong way!" she coughed. "Nearly exploded!"

"What the coffee or what Jonas said?" Keith asked with a laugh. Molly did not respond as she wiped coffee from her chin, not being able to hold back her smile.

"I think the cup would still fall. I've never seen a cup that doesn't fall when you drop it, so it'd fall for sure," Bruce said.

"But there's no gravity. That's what we're saying. You don't get it," Jonas said.

Bruce thought for a minute. "Well, with no gravity it would float. And, then drift off to the Moon because that would still have gravity."

"And if there was coffee in the cup what would that do?" Jonas asked expectantly.

"It would run out to the ground if it tipped, just like you said."

"Now Moll, tell us what you think?" Jonas asked as he pushed his empty coffee cup towards the middle of the table.

"You guys have all the answers, so why do I need to say anything. Finished have we? Let's go Bruce, I've got shopping to do. I can't waste my time listening to you lot and your hypothetical arguments about gravity."

"Typical! Start a serious scientific debate and what happens," Jonas said exasperatedly. "She just wants to up and leave because she spouts a few facts, thinks she's clever and then pisses off. They know when they're licked. Women! Never understand them, and they'll never understand me."

"You're right Jonas. You may not know about gravity or spilling coffee on the Moon, but you're dead right when it comes to women," Molly said as she stood and collected her handbag from the back of her chair. "You paying or did your wallet float to the Moon too?"

Game Boy

Gaming is extremely popular on a global scale providing stimulation and entertainment to millions. To play well demands intellectual ability, sharp reflexes and intense concentration. Individuals fight digital battles for victory or defeat; they make friends and build teams. If only political and religious wars could be fought in similar, less violent and destructive ways - but alas there is little chance of that happening! To see a live performance by a gamer is entertaining and enlightening. A non-gamer can become intrigued and engrossed, or appalled by watching such a performance, but to a gamer playing is a drug, addictive and essential.

His eyes focus attentively on the screen and his finger repeatedly clicks the mouse button. He is oblivious to his environment, his concentration focused solely on winning the game on the computer monitor. At twenty-three and a recent university graduate his thoughts are on inventing a computer game appropriate for universal players who would pay to play, making him rich. Now though, his thoughts are on the immediate challenge of the game he is playing.

He squirms on his seat, and adjusts his position to see well. He kicks the desk inadvertently bumping a cold cup of coffee he made spilling brown liquid across the desk. He does not notice it run slowly to the edge of the desk and drop into a dark expanding pool on the floor.

He sniffles, but cannot hear himself because of the thump-thump-thump of music in his ears. His IPod plays music loudly; background accompaniment to stimulate his brain.

He picks his nose and rubs the snot on his trouser leg. He sucks his finger. Uncomfortable again, he moves his chair back and leans closer to the screen while his finger works the mouse button feverishly. His gaze is unbroken; he rarely blinks in case he might miss a key clue or opportunity.

His left hand disappears inside his trousers adjusting his twisted scrotum. He sways back in his chair to fondle his penis, the excitement of the game arousing his sensuality. His right hand busily clicks away as he moves the cursor to specific points just in time to score points. He retracts his hand and rubs his nose.

He sniffles. The noise in his ears changes to Beethoven's 5th Symphony, but he doesn't notice the difference; his concentration high on music and the cursor. He rocks back again on his chair, then moves the chair forward as he finds he is too far from the screen. His feet tuck under the chair as he lurches anxiously at the screen.

His face changes tension. He screws his face up as the stress of the game begins to take its toll. He sways to one side and then the other to maximize control over the mouse. The spilt coffee is now in a small pool on the floor.

He sniffs loudly, rubs his nose with the back of his hand and continues the onslaught of his internet opponent. He is winning, but needs to keep his focus or he fears he will lose. He slides his chair back and stretches his legs out in front kicking the power cable and threatening to dislodge the cord so his desktop computer will turn off.

Beethoven's Fifth rings in his ears. His brain, saturated with distractions and working furiously at concentrating on the game is at its peak. Adrenalin rushes through his body. This is the 'high' he seeks, wants, needs - the thrill is intense. His hand returns to his scrotum and penis in exciting anticipation of the foreseeable win. He leans back, enjoying the thrill of the game and his own stimulation.

Suddenly he lurches closer to the screen. His hand withdraws from his pants to rub his nose. He sniffs again loudly. Pinching his nose to stop a sneeze he plays on without noticing the onlookers who stare at this amazing spectacle in action. He runs his fingers through his hair.

Nearing the climax of the game, he pulls the chair closer to the screen and kicks his feet out in front. Then he changes position again, turns the chair a little on its side all the while maintaining sharp focus on the screen. He rubs his forehead, but there is no perspiration.

He wins. His face, now close to the screen glares gloatingly into his opponents eyes. His left hand jabs the air, fist clenched. He pumps it skywards showing excitement at his success, like a golfer does after sinking a lengthy putt on the last hole to win a championship. Enthralled he gesticulates at the screen and points at his score.

The throng of spectators, who had gathered around sighs collectively, then drifts off just as he looks up from the screen. He sniffs loudly just as the IPod grows silent.

Embarrassed, he flushes red and looks sheepishly for somewhere to hide. There is nowhere. He sits silently looking at the screen until he is alone. He begins another game.

Several stories relate to mineral exploration in Mongolia.

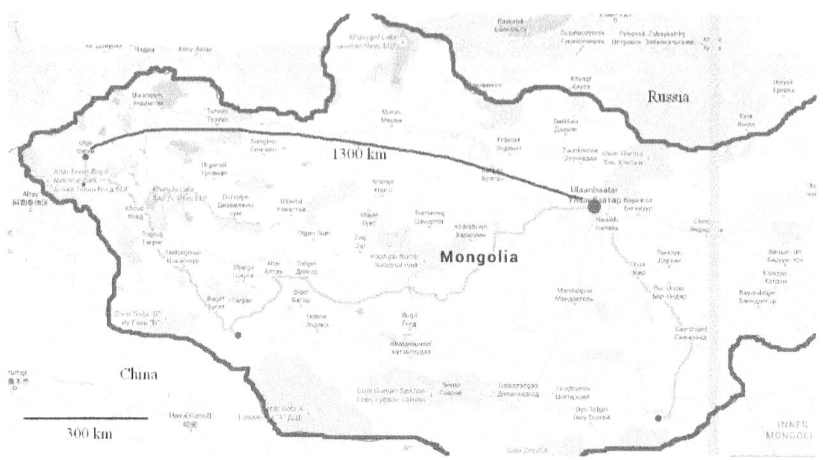

Map of Mongolia showing the flight from Ulaanbaatar to Ölgii in the western part of the country. Also shown is the route taken to return to the capital and then to start a drilling program in the south eastern Gobi Desert.

Gers in the wintry landscape of the Gobi Desert.

The Mongolian Fire Worker

A stressed voice yells "Bargii! Bargii! Bargii!"

Bargii, a young man of medium height, slight build and boyish appearance rushes from behind a white ger to the source of the voice (A traditional Mongolian ger or yurt is a portable, round tent covered with skins or felt and used as a dwelling by nomadic groups in the steppes of Central Asia). The camp manager calls instructions about making a fire in one of the gers. The balmy autumn days have ended abruptly and an icy Arctic blast gusts across the treeless South Gobi Desert, making the gers cold and uncomfortable for the workers.

A band of geologists and their catering crew are camped on a stony plain in two rows of off-white gers. A double ger links the kitchen to a mess where everyone eats. Another ger stands apart from the rest. It houses a flush toilet and shower for the Europeans. A wooden outhouse built over a pit forms the ablution for the Mongolian workers. All doorways, low, decorated and wooden face southeast towards the rising sun and away from the prevailing wind.

Bargii is always busy and nicknamed "Duracell" by one of the geologists, to everyone's amusement. He wears a grey baseball-type cap with Sharf written across the front. Usually he twists it to the right side and tilts it back from his face. Bargii only speaks Mongolian, so is oblivious to the joke. The first person to wake and the last to bed, Bargii provides an essential service apart from his other chores; fire worker.

Each ger has a metal stove, roughly in the shape of a small pig. It stands on four metal legs above the floor in the centre of the ger. A flue pipe runs upright through the round roof of the ger from the nostrils of the metal pig. The rear end of the pig has a flap through which Bargii lights and stokes the fire. A circular lid with a handle opens in the flat top to allow access for adding wood and coal. A tray slides from under the belly of the pig and catches ash. It needs emptying regularly.

Bargii's task is to light and maintain the fires in all the gers. He becomes upset if someone decides they should light a fire for themselves. It is 'his' job and it reflects badly on his performance if other people interfere or do it for him. This happened one day when a European visitor, feeling cold, started to load wood and dried dung into the stove in the office ger. Bargii heard the characteristic squeak of the rear flap opening and the sound of dried fuel dropping into the metal box, and came running. He waved his arms about furiously, shouted abusively, but did not swear (the Mongolian language is gentle not vulgar) and pushed the fire-lighting culprit away from the stove. A translator informed the perpetrator of the insult to Bargii, reminding them it was Bargii's job and not the foreigner to light the fire.

During cold days Bargii is continuously active. He periodically cleans ashes from the stoves otherwise they fill and are ineffective. He makes new fires using scarce dry wood and dried animal dung supplied by the nomad who lives nearby. Scavenged scraps of paper, cardboard and plastic help to start a fire. Once the wood and dung are burning, he adds coal from Tsagaan Tolgoi, a mine in the neighbouring district, referred to as an Aimag.

Adding the right amount of coal is an art form because too much coal dampens and extinguishes the fire. The right amount produces abundant heat enabling workers inside to strip off the outer layer of clothing and perspire in the hot, dry environment. Sometimes it is too hot and they swing the door open to allow cold air to circulate and reduce the heat. Clouds of fine ash float in the air as Bargii pours powdered and granulated coal onto the flames. He smiles, points to his jacket zipper and by his motions indicates the workers will soon unzip their jackets and strip off to enjoy the heat. He smiles again. They all smile and say, "Баярлалаа!"

Bargii also fills water barrels and helps load and unload them from the trailer. The water gathering system is simple. He puts four large empty blue plastic containers on a trailer, then wheels the trailer across the flat stony ground, down a gentle slope and across a dry stream bed to a water well. The shallow well is in granite near a fault line, acting as an aquifer. It recharges slowly. A wooden hatch covers the well, preventing birds and animals from accidentally falling in. Bargii takes a metal bucket and rope and lowers it a metre or two to fill it with water. Pulling the bucket up requires some strength, but as he has done it many times, it comes easily. Repeating the actions, he fills each container. Bargii is smart. He realised on the first day it is easier to leave the empty containers on the trailer and fill them there rather than put them on the ground near the well and then try to lift the heavy load back onto the trailer once he had filled them. One of the vehicles with a towing hitch takes the water trailer back to camp where Bargii unloads the barrels.

Again, Bargii's cleverness stands out. Each container has a black plastic lid secured by a metal strap. Instead of lifting the containers out he 'walks' them to the edge of the trailer, tilts them so they slide then he slips them quickly onto the ground making sure to stop them crashing onto their sides and spilling the precious liquid. He does this with the help of a fellow worker.

When he greets other workers he smiles, winks or gives a thumbs up sign. Bargii walks with rapid short steps in boots covering his calves. He is a happy person who regularly hums the chorus to a popular song, "Sanaj amirlah ijiia." It's about someone who has lost their mother and they lament her passing.

In periods of high wind, Bargii shows his expertise in stabilising the gers. He fills sand bags with dirt dug and piled to make the cesspit then carries them on his back to where he thinks they are needed. He lashes a bag to a rope, then throws the rope directly across the ger to the other side. Repeating the bag filling and carrying, he ties another bag to the other end of the rope and pulls hard on it to lift the bags off the ground. The two bags weigh the ger down and prevent it blowing away.

Another trick Bargii uses to stabilise the gers and reduce dust blowing inside is to scrape and push loose rock and soil into a mound against the outside wall of each ger. He makes a low retaining wall to stop strong gusts from blowing under the ger and lifting it off the ground.

An observant Bargii saved a ger from catching fire. The office ger contained computers and other electronic devices, mainly to charge them up. The power outlets to several computers had failed when the new generator sent hundreds of Watts through the lines before the system had been tested. Subsequently a voltage regulator was connected to prevent damage to the devices. It had been purchased at the black market in Ulaanbaatar. An office worker had fitted it to control the voltage and current to the equipment, preventing surges and spikes from the diesel generator located on the outskirts of the camp.

Returning to the office after breakfast one day a geologist encountered an overpowering and sickening foul smelling odour. Immediately he called Bargii thinking he had placed poor quality dried dung in the stove as fuel. The geologist gesticulated, trying to explain the problem. Bargii initially took offence, thinking he was to blame for the stench. He stoked the fire, lifted the lid and inspected the contents. It all seemed fine; thumbs up! Bargii grabbed a water container and poured water on the stove believing the welding might be too hot. Suddenly he leapt back, shouting and pointing at the toxic plume of gases rising rapidly from the overheating electrical regulator. He quickly pulled out the electrical plug, carried the fuming device out of the office then placed it down wind of the doorway. He stood to watch the fumes continue to rise from the metal box. Returning to the ger he tied the door open despite the cold wind blowing strongly from the northwest so the electrical fumes would escape amidst the swirling air. A hero for a short time Bargii smiled at the appreciative comments then turned and went back to his regular chores.

Bargii is learning to speak English. He greets people with "Good Morning." He smiles and holds out his fingers like a child learning to count. Numbers one to ten are fine, but he struggles with the teen numbers to twenty, saying 'ten' as in "fif ten."

A negative side to Bargii is his dislike of ravens. He throws stones at them when they land inside the camp. A rubbish pit is a great place for pickings so the ravens swoop down looking for a tasty snack. Their quick eye warns them when to take flight as a stone from Bargii hurtles in their direction.

Around the camp the catch-cry of "Bargii! Bargii! Bargii!" rings out again as the sun sinks low in the reddish sky. Fires need lighting. Duracell is on the move again, running to get his bucket and fuel from the coal and wood dump. The day ends as it starts, "Bargii! Bargii! Bargii!" He is the most popular man in Mongolia.

Cheminis Lodge, Virginiatown, Canada

It is the place where I'm staying while managing a diamond drilling program in Ontario, Canada. The company I'm working for is exploring their tenement for gold. Bonnie Devine and Dave French run Cheminis Lodge. Bonnie was married previously but is divorced. Her first husband died a few years ago.

Dave is slightly younger and has lived all his life in Vtown, he calls it, not Virginiatown. He has travelled as far west as Thunder Bay and has seen the Atlantic Ocean around Prince Edward Island. He drives machinery for the Kirkland Lake County and used to drive snow ploughs in winter. He smokes. His corroded teeth have gaps between brown stained residual prongs. He talks with a hesitation, saying things like, "I was telling her about, err- hum, what I meant to say, err- hum, I was telling her about, err-hum....I saw a moose carcass. err-hum, on the side of the road. Did you see it? Err-hum, it shouldn't've been there. Err the season's over."

Bonnie must be in her late sixties. She is tall, about 5'10" (178 cm) with short straight grey hair cropped close to her head. She wears glasses. Bonnie's a talker with a great welcoming smile and penetrating gaze. She almost burnt the house down just after I arrived. She had left a pan of fat on the hotplate and it caught fire. Bonnie wandered through the house carrying the hot pot, panicking. Not knowing what to do she dropped the flaming pan in the sink and turned on the tap. Flames shot up to the ceiling, causing blackening. Luckily, Paul, another resident who was standing nearby grabbed a tea towel and, ignoring the flames, held it under the tap briefly before dropping it over the incendiary pot.

Dave usually cooks breakfast and Bonnie makes dinner. The meals are basic English fare. Eggs cooked in different ways and toast is Dave's menu. The last two nights Bonnie has cooked roast pork and roast chicken with coleslaw, mashed potatoes, and peas. Nothing exotic or extravagant.

My offsider or field assistant is Bernie Sampson. He is 72 years old and lives on the dge of the tenement. He helped the previous geologist clear and mark out the drilling pads prior to arrival of the drilling rig. He is about 5'10" (178 cm) with dark straight hair, bifocals and a grinning face. To give you a clue about his sense of humour he told me a joke. Minutes after we had met he asked a question.

"Do you know why Jesus was not born in Québec?"

I shook my head.

"They couldn't find a virgin or three wise men."

He roared with laughter. Then he followed up with a comment on Dave's weak coffee.

"It's like making love in a canoe: fucking close to water."

He also described a difficult time he was having nailing some wood. "It was like a dog fucking a football!"

He will have been married for 50 years on January 16 to Connie. I was fortunate to meet her. She is about 5'6" (168 cm) with short blonde hair. Her roundish face perches on a small body and she is always on the go. She works the computer at their house and corresponds with their three sons and one daughter using email. Bernie knows about computers, but leaves it to Connie to use.

Losing it.

Killing me softly with his song was playing on the radio as Tom Waterhouse; a government geologist strode to the front door of apartment 13 in a row of cement Besser block rental units in Shepherd Street, Darwin. The louvred windows were open to catch the morning breeze. A vacuum cleaner started inside the apartment just as Tom knocked on the door. He stood and waited. He figured nobody would hear his knocking over the sound of the vacuum. His friends expected him, so he tried the handle. The door opened easily. On entering, he saw his friend Dick in a pair of old white rugby shorts and bare-barrel chest working the vacuum cleaner across the tiled floor. Dick spotted Tom and stopped working. *Strumming my pain with his fingers* played in the background as Dick shook his hand.

"I'll be done in a few minutes," he said. "Mary's in the kitchen. Go through."

Tom went up two steps onto a short landing and through a narrow passage to the kitchen and meals area. Mary was washing dishes at the sink after a late breakfast. The whirr of the vacuum started up again as Tom reached the kitchen. Tom and Mary greeted each other politely and did not shake hands, kiss or hug. They were friends, but working in the same office for the government meant they shared mutual respect for each other with a slight stiffness, following the traditional protocol between work colleagues. The noise from the vacuum made conversation difficult, so Tom sat in one of two chairs at the table on which were copies of the Northern

Territory News and the Weekend Australian. Instead of reading the papers he studied Mary.

Mary was English and she and her husband, Dick had migrated under a scheme allowing them to come to Australia for ten pounds in the days before Australia changed to decimal currency. Dick was a civil engineer for the Works Department. He was short and stocky with a thick, muscular neck and roundish face. His robust frame hinted at weight lifting or wrestling as a hobby, but he was a rugby league player. Mary was slightly taller than Dick and very attractive, a reason Tom was watching her closely as she put dirty breakfast plates in a sink full of hot soapy water. She was a clerk and shared the accounting and pay office with another woman in the geological branch of the government office where Tom worked. Her conspicuously large firm breasts on a well-proportioned body appealed to Tom; he was mesmerised and entranced watching Mary's body move effortless at the sink. She had tied her auburn hair in a loose bun at the back of her head. Her long white neck supported an attractive perpetually smiling face. Even without makeup, Mary was agreeable to the eye. The vacuum continued whirring in the background and the plates clicked together in the sink. She turned and smiled at Tom. He glanced away embarrassed because she had caught him staring.

The whirring ceased and only the radio played in the background. A commentator announced an advertisement for a new car dealership. Dick had finished cleaning and appeared at the end of the corridor, holding the vacuum. He opened a tall cupboard and stowed the cleaner inside. Walking to the fridge, he asked Tom if he wanted a beer. Tom nodded, and Dick reached inside the fridge and took out two cans of VB.

"It's only ten, you guys," Mary cautioned. "Getting an early start are we?"

Dick did not answer and sat with Tom at the table. They pulled the rings to open the cans and then after clinking them together, swallowed mouthfuls of cold beer. Beads of perspiration ran down Dick's face. His hairy chest was damp with sweat. He took another large gulp. Tom had switched his gaze to Dick and starting talking about the events of the week. They talked about local politics, management of the apartment complex and the Saturday sports results. The Sydney Rabbitohs had beaten Parramatta and Dick was pleased.

The second beer disappeared as fast as the first and then he and Mary went to their bedroom to change clothes. Tom waited in the kitchen and slowly finished his beer. He scanned the newspapers looking for articles to read, and not finding any of interest stood to stretch his legs. He dropped his empty can of beer in the disposal bin. Dick packed his sporting bag with his boots, socks, towel and the red and green Rabbitoh's jersey. They were going to Richardson Park for the regular Sunday rugby league competition and today the Rabbitohs would play Brothers.

The '72 Holden Premier in the parking area started easily and Dick reversed it into the street. Mary sat in the front with Dick and Tom in the back behind Mary. They drove a short distance to the drive-in bottle department of the Palm Hotel, so Tom could buy a case of Four X beer. Then they headed to the sports ground. Dick found a parking spot under a Banyan tree and they walked from there to the entrance, paid a fee and found a viewing spot with other Rabbitoh's fans on the crest of a mound overlooking the southern end of the oval near the toilet block. The third grade game was in progress. The trio bought meat pies from a supporter's stand nearby and Tom washed his down with a beer.

Later the same afternoon Dick left them to change before taking to the field with his mates. The Brothers team, in white with thin black stripes, played well against the red and greens, but could not overtake the score raised by some excellent ball handling and aggressive running from the back line of the Rabbitohs. Dick was instrumental in scoring one of three tries. At the end of the match, the players showered, dressed and drank the last few cans of Tom's beer before they drove to Andy Brown's flat in Nightcliff. Andy was a friend of Dick's. On the way, they stopped to buy a six-pack of VB, Dick's favourite beer and a bottle of Riesling for Mary.

Most of the team, their wives and girlfriends had arrived when they walked in. Someone had bought several large pizzas and slices were disappearing fast as the hungry men ate and drank to satisfy their needs. Talking in small groups, they discussed unsuccessful rugby moves and ways they might improve their game. They stirred each other about dropped passes and missed opportunities. Wives talked of children and school, issues of health and planned holidays down south. Camaraderie was strong, reflecting successful team spirit, mate ship and prolonged bonding. People began leaving when all the food and drinks were gone. It was late, about eleven when Dick, Mary and Tom left accompanied by Andy and Kathleen, and Darrell and Jocelyn. Mary wanted to see Jocelyn and Kathleen's new apartment, so the group departed in separate cars and drove to Parap.

Jocelyn and Kathleen were primary school teachers from New South Wales. They had signed a government contract to teach for three years with special benefits: an annual return flight to Sydney amongst them. They met at their school and moved in together to reduce expenses of renting single accommodation after spending months at the government hostel where Tom was living. Their boyfriends, Andy and Darrell played rugby league with Dick. Andy worked in a bank and Darrell was a surveyor's assistant.

Darrell and Jocelyn were arguing when Dick, Mary and Tom arrived. It seemed Jocelyn was unhappy with Darrell's behaviour. He had said something about teachers to Jocelyn's annoyance and she was giving him a tongue-lashing. They stopped bickering when the others walked in. Jocelyn focused on showing Mary around while the men continued chatting about the game they had just finished. Later, when Dick wanted to leave he could not see Mary, so asked Tom to go and find her while he went for a leak. Tom found Mary and Jocelyn in a bedroom, with Jocelyn tearfully explaining to Mary the breakup of her relationship with Darrell. Tom apologised for interrupting and informed Mary why he had been looking for her. Mary left the room and then Jocelyn and Tom took turns explaining who they were and what they were doing in Darwin. Their conversation was interrupted by Mary, who came back to tell Tom she and Dick were leaving. They said goodbye and departed for home and bed. It was past midnight.

Weeks later, on a Friday evening as the sun set over the Arafura Sea, Tom and Jocelyn met by chance outside the Don Hotel in Cavenagh Street. Jocelyn had been drinking with other school teachers and had walked onto the street from the cocktail bar just as Tom strode by on his way to meet Dick at the RSL club. They chatted briefly during which Jocelyn mentioned an upcoming dance festival. She invited Tom to join a group of teachers who planned attending the following Friday night. Tom agreed and handed Jocelyn a business card with his telephone number, so she could call him with the details.

The following week Tom was excited about the dance festival. He thought about Jocelyn and what a lovely bright woman she was and the enjoyment he felt in the brief moments they had spent talking. He wondered who else would attend; Kathleen obviously and probably her boyfriend Andy, but he did not know anybody else.

Unexpectedly, another school teacher at his hostel asked him to go with her to the festival. He had been standing in line waiting for his evening meal when a tall brunette, wearing beige riding jodhpurs, pale blue and brown boots rushed alongside. Tom turned to see who it was. Her flushed face, red from sun exposure, bore beads of perspiration. They clung precipitously to her forehead.

"Where did you leave your horse?" Tom cheekily said, noticing she had not changed out of her riding clothes.

"On the dude ranch."

"Get the day off?"

"No just took an early afternoon."

They shuffled along the line towards the serving area, picking up a plate each as they sidled along.

"You're late today," she said.

"Had a couple of beers," Tom replied. "How come you know? Have you been watching me?"

"Of course. I watch all the handsome men here."

"Keep you pretty busy then!"

"No, not really. There's just you and another bloke, but he smokes and I don't like cigarette smoke. It makes me sneeze."

"Remind me not to take it up then," Tom stated, looking her in the eyes.

"You'll miss your turn if you're not careful," she said.

Tom looked toward the line and realised it had moved, and he had not. There was now a gap and a server was waiting to pile food on his plate.

Tom took his plate of steak, chips and beans, picked up cutlery and a napkin and looked for a place to sit. Empty chairs and tables were available at this late dinner period. He spotted one close by and sat. Almost immediately, the woman wearing jodhpurs sat opposite.

"Want a drink?" she asked.

"Yes, thanks. Water will be fine."

Returning to the table, carrying two glasses brimming with cold water, she said her name was Ailsa. Tom was about to tell her his name but before he could utter a syllable she said.

"I know yours. It's Tom isn't it?"

"Well, you are full of surprises. You've been spying on me, and I didn't know. How long has this been going on?"

Ailsa laughed and talked candidly about observing him ever since he had arrived. She explained it was the first opportunity she had to meet him, so she was going to make the most of it. Filled with energy and confidence from the spirited horse ride Ailsa felt uninhibited and excited. They ate and talked until the doors of the dining room closed. Walking out together, they continued their conversation. Tom followed Ailsa to her room. Ailsa's room was on the top floor of a three story apartment complex adjacent to Mitchell Street. It faced west and with the window screens open it caught the sea breeze cooling the room during summer. A ubiquitous ceiling fan rotated slowly, circulating a weak down draft of cooling air. Ailsa offered Tom a beer from a small refrigerator tucked under a desk. She took one too and then sat on her bed with her back against the wall. Tom sat uncomfortably in a plastic chair near the desk. They looked at each other silently until Ailsa asked Tom whether he liked music.

Swallowing his beer hurriedly, he nervously replied his taste was catholic and anything she wanted to play would be suitable.

"What do like?" he asked.

"This is my favourite at the moment," she said rolling across her bed to press play on the tape deck at the head of her bed.

Roberta Flack began singing *Killing me softly*.

"I like this one," Tom said with a smile.

They listened until it had finished playing. Ailsa rolled her body along the bed so she could press the stop button. Instead of rolling back to where she had been sitting she slid across the edge of the bed and looked Tom in the eye.

"Put the beer down and come and lay down with me," she wistfully said, holding out her hand to grasp his.

Surprised by the sudden change in her demeanour and the situation he was now in Tom followed her instructions and stretched out alongside her as she wiggled backwards on the bed to make room. She flung her arm around his neck and kissed him hard on the mouth. Tom returned the kiss with enthusiasm and excitement, and a hardening sensation rapidly grew inside his pants. He lost focus on kissing Ailsa and worried about a premature ejaculation from his swelling penis. She detected his seeming disinterest and pulling away, said, "Anything wrong?"

"No. I'm just taken a bit by surprise. We only met twenty minutes ago," Tom said timidly.

"I guess I was a bit aggressive, but you are so handsome and sexy and I've wanted to do that since I first saw you. I just had to do it. That's all. I couldn't resist the temptation any longer. Do you want me to stop?"

"No."

In an instant, Ailsa thrust her lips at Tom's mouth. Embracing tightly she continued her intense kissing. He could not resist. Locked in a passionate embrace Tom felt his essence begin oozing from his rock hard penis. He could not stop it despite concentrating with every effort to get his brain to switch off the steady slow seepage of semen.

Ailsa was ecstatic. She had dreamed of this moment for weeks and now she was enjoying every second of his warm luscious kisses. Her heart raced and her body ached. She felt it was too soon to rip his shirt and trousers off and make passionate love. Her emotions cried out for satisfaction, but her head was content with long breathtaking kisses. Ailsa's head won her internal conflict. She released her arms from his neck, rolled back on the bed and faced the ceiling. Breathing heavily she gasped.

"That was terrific. You are a wonderful kisser. We'll have to do it again another time."

Tom was relieved they had stopped kissing. His heart also pumped rapidly and he gasped for air. Tom faced an internal problem of his own, reducing his erection so it would not be obvious when he stood up. He tried relaxing by focusing on breathing deeply with his eyes closed. They lay side by side listening to each other's breath. Minutes passed. When Tom felt he had regained control he reluctantly said he should be going because he had things to organise for the next day. Ailsa nodded understandably. She also had materials to prepare for her class. Tom bent over and gave Ailsa one long last kiss before he stood, adjusted his softening erection in his pants, felt a damp spot near the fly and walked to the door. Ailsa followed him and said she would like to see him again soon. They kissed hard before Tom walked gingerly down the corridor and stairs, and back to his room, aware of a dark wet spot on his trousers. He was annoyed with himself for losing control yet he was also elated for having an attractive woman throw herself eagerly into his life. Perhaps she could open his heart to new adventures.

As the days passed, the more Tom thought about what had happened the more concerned he became. He was in a quandary. Jocelyn had invited him to the dance festival and he had been seeing Ailsa almost daily since they had exchanged intense kisses in her room. He did not know how to handle the situation dealing with two women. What could he say; he liked them both. Procrastination rarely pays dividends because of missed opportunities, but Tom had luck on his side even though he did not know it. Jocelyn and Ailsa knew one another, as school teachers they socialised as a group and drank cocktails at the Don Hotel. They had been talking about the festival and about Tom. Keen rivalry ensued between the two women for his affection. Tom, at an apex of a relationship triangle never imagined or realised the intensity of the forces competing for his attention. Jocelyn and Ailsa arranged for several couples to join them in a group so they would meet Tom at the hostel. They would walk to the dance festival only a few blocks away.

Saturday night of the dance festival arrived without a cloud in the sky. A gentle sea breeze blew from the northwest. In the morning, Tom had ironed a shirt then hung it with a pair of brown trousers. He cleaned his brown shoes and gently stuffed a pair of beige socks inside. He had then walked to the newsagency to buy a newspaper, stopped at a coffee shop for a flat white and had read the paper. After a light lunch, he slept beneath a cooling fan. As the yellow sun sank over the Arafura Sea and those who watched it saw a green flash Tom shaved and took a shower in the communal ablution block. A splash of aftershave brought tingling stings to his skin where the razor had made small nicks. He dressed. Checking his appearance in the mirror he thought about the impending entertainment and what might happen. Apprehension filled his mind. He felt anxious about a possible conflict erupting between Jocelyn and Ailsa. Tom was tense and nervous, yet excited and enthusiastic about the dance festival. Just have fun and enjoy yourself, and let events unfold naturally, he said to himself as he opened the door and walked into the corridor.

Tom met Ailsa as she was stepping down the stairs from her apartment. She wore a cotton print dress with a tropical pattern of palms and blue ocean, and a pale blue blouse with V-neck and ruffles at the ends of the short sleeves. A turquoise necklace hung loosely across her chest. Tom said she looked stunning, which she did. A slight crimson blush rushed to her cheeks acknowledging his compliment. They linked arms and walked to a parking area at the side of the building where a group of men and women stood talking. Jocelyn was there. As they approached, the group turned to gaze at them. Tom and Ailsa stepped lightly and happily towards them. Jocelyn greeted Tom with a firm kiss. Not to be outdone, Ailsa immediately kissed Tom squarely on the mouth. Hoots erupted from several men in the group. Tom laughed before suggesting they leave. Everybody had arrived.

Led by Tom, bearing Jocelyn on one arm and Ailsa on the other the group made its way to the plaza where the dance festival was starting. A band had assembled on a temporary stage overlooking an expansive wooden dance floor. The musicians were tuning their instruments while technicians busily tested the lighting and sound effects. Three bars serving alcohol and run by the Don, Victoria and Darwin hotels served drinks. The group made its way to the Don bar, their favourite hotel to buy drinks.

The band started playing and the group enthusiastically joined others on the dance floor. Soon the floor was jammed with dancers. There was barely room to move, so each dance brought the dancers eye to eye. Ailsa and Jocelyn took turns dancing with Tom. He had no time to stand and drink. Only when the band stopped for a break was he able to sit and enjoy a beer. Meanwhile the rest of the group enjoyed carousing, becoming increasingly drunk and boisterous as the night passed. A slow waltz played to end the festival and Tom had a difficult choice. Dance with Ailsa or Jocelyn? The turn belonged to Jocelyn, so she and Tom wrapped arms around each other, slowly stepped repeatedly back and forth, then sideways. Cheek to cheek in the moonlight they waltzed until the music stopped. Jocelyn gave Tom a long tongue-penetrating kiss. It sent nerve tingling shivers along his spine, resulting in unrestrained penile hardening. Fortunately, in the darkness Tom was able to walk from the stage while adjusting his pants to reposition his erection without anyone noticing.

Ailsa and the group had left the festival before the music had stopped. Tom and Jocelyn found themselves alone. They looked around and not seeing their friends, walked with small groups of inebriated revellers and couples strolling arm in arm back to the hostel. Hand in hand they walked while discussing the music they had just heard, people they saw and the events of the coming weeks. Tom informed Jocelyn he was leaving on Monday to spend six weeks at a geological bush camp alongside of Jim Jim Creek. If she wanted to visit on a weekend he would inform Mary and the two of them could arrange the necessary travel details. She thought it a great idea because she had not been outside of Darwin since arriving there a year ago.

They arrived at the hostel car park where Jocelyn had left her red and black Mini Cooper. One last kiss ended an exhilarating night for them both. As she started the car, Jocelyn said she would talk to Mary about arranging a visit to his camp. Then she was gone. Tom walked exhausted to his room. As he undressed his feet felt sore and his legs weary. He had never danced so much in all his life.

Three weeks later, on a Saturday afternoon a car stopped outside the long brown marquee where the camping geologists ate their meals. Mary and Jocelyn alighted from the vehicle and met Campbell Macgregor, the boss of the Jim Jim camp. They exchanged greetings and Mary unloaded a cardboard box containing mail and administrative papers. Macgregor explained they only had a small single person tent available for visitors because a senior public servant occupied the larger tent. He suggested Mary could use the small tent and as Jocelyn had specifically travelled to see Tom, they could work out their own sleeping arrangements. Macgregor said he would talk with Tom before dinner.

Macgregor had established his geological base camp on the western bank of a series of large elongate billabongs making up the Jim Jim Creek so his team of geologists could carry out a regional geological survey. He proudly showed the women all the facilities, including a hot water shower, toilet, kitchen and office. Macgregor explained how they heated water from lighting a fire beneath a 44-gallon drum and having gravity feed water to it from another drum positioned high in a nearby tree. A pump on the bank of the billabong supplied water to the upper tank. The camp of eight men could all take hot showers without the supply running out. He would ensure there was adequate hot water for them to take showers before they ate.

At dinner, Mary and Jocelyn met everyone. Conversations focused on events in Darwin and the rest of the world because the men had not seen a newspaper since leaving town. Macgregor spoke to Tom about the sleeping arrangements for the next two nights – a public holiday in Darwin meant the women would leave camp after breakfast on Monday. Macgregor also reminded Tom it was his responsibility to entertain Jocelyn. Tom said he had a task he wanted to complete and might be able to achieve it with Jocelyn's help. He would also take her fishing for barramundi. Satisfied with the arrangements Macgregor joined the others at dinner. Tom went for a shower before returning to the mess tent.

Later the same evening when the conversations became wearisome Tom escorted Jocelyn to his tent. He explained he would sleep in the large visitor's tent so she could get a good night's sleep on the single wire-framed bed and soft mattress in his tent. She looked perplexed, but did not say anything and sat on the bed. As there was nowhere else to sit, Tom sat alongside. They talked about their work, the drive out from Darwin and the next day's activities. Soon they were lying together on the bed embracing and kissing. The sagging narrow bed brought them close together without any effort. Being up close to a curvaceous attractive woman and feeling intense pleasure from the continual amorous bond inevitably stirred Tom's proclivity for sexual arousal. He knew what was happening, but in the confines of his tent he did not care – he was enraptured.

A steady seepage of semen oozed from his throbbing penis. It spread across his khaki shorts and developed into a massive wet patch. He only realised it once they had stood so Jocelyn could use the toilet. Back in bed Jocelyn took control. Soon they were in rhythmical copulation, but the pleasure dissipated rapidly because Tom soon reached uncontrollable climax. Jocelyn was disappointed and frustrated, and rolling over suggested Tom sleep in the visitor's tent as he had originally intended. He quickly dressed and walked with great elation and satisfaction down the slope and across the flat to the visitor's tent where he slept contentedly on a spare bed.

Jocelyn was in a foul mood the following morning and her tenor remained the same all day. The lovers went fishing and she caught two barramundi using a hand line and lures. For the rest of the day they traced an overgrown track through grass and savannah woodland until they lost it where it crossed a wide clearing. Unable to pick up the track on the other side of the clearing they stopped their search. Tom lit a fire and cooked the fish for lunch.

That night the two lovers tossed and turned in the single bed and had sex at Jocelyn's pleasure. Eventually, exhausted and craving sleep they slept fitfully and uncomfortably until dawn. After breakfast, Jocelyn and Mary said farewell and departed for Darwin. The men teased Tom incessantly about his amorous nightly adventures, but Tom just smiled, ignoring their crude remarks.

Jocelyn never returned to Tom's camp and they did not see one another again. Even when Tom went to Darwin on his break. Word had reached Jocelyn Tom had lost his virginity to her. Presumably the gossip came from Mary, but possibly it was a rumour spread by another school teacher during her visit to the bush camp. News about Jocelyn was she eloped with a cattle rancher from Western Australia before the end of the school year.

Ailsa and Tom dated several times in Darwin, but his long absences made a meaningful relationship impossible. Though Tom always remembered the night with Jocelyn in the tent on the banks of the billabong he regretted not making a greater effort with Ailsa. Losing his virginity was Tom's initiation into the world of women and sex. Telling me about it one night in Canberra when he was drunk was my full introduction into his world.

(Tom died of leukaemia in 2018. He never saw Jocelyn again and only saw Ailsa twice in Canberra).

Grey Skies, Drizzle and Rainbows

A story related by Tom.

She took another sip from her glass and tasted the rich fruity flavours of the red liquor. Looking out the dirty window to the passing traffic she reflected on her day. The sun rose brightly as normal, but something seemed different in the pattern of pink clouds floating in bands far to the west. Then she realised it was over, her relationship with Ted, and her life was starting again.

She had met Ted on a train heading west and they had talked for hours, finding common threads in apparently dissimilar lives. They shared family stories without going into depth, empathised about troubled times and laughed at funny predicaments. Time flew. At the end of the journey they missed each other's company, wishing they had continued their conversation. It never happened, or did it. Had she dreamed about Ted? Was he an imaginary friend or had it really happened.

Another sip and the aroma of the swilled wine tantalised her palate. His hands had wandered across her body, delighting and giving great pleasure. No other man had done it to her, well not so gently and lovingly. His hands were different; caressing and feeling, not rough and grasping. His light touch tingled and tickled making her shiver. She asked him to stop. Regretting her quick remark, now she wished he had continued. Why had she said it?

The view through the glass was of traffic moving slowly towards the intersection. The occasional pedestrian hurried against the wind before the drizzle turned to steady rain. Grey skies broke into patchy clouds and sunlight tried to find its way to earth. Rays of light poked through gaps in the clouds. She glimpsed part of a rainbow. Drops of rain splashed on the window. She turned to her glass seeking solace at the loss of a friend.

He had picked up on her melancholic mood; her voice seemed stuck in her throat, an unusual event because normally she was talkative, lighthearted, and engaging. Why had she changed? She blamed Ted. He had not reacted and spoken as she had expected. He had not held her or come to her bed the previous night. They had not spoken in the morning except in clipped expressions. It had led to confusion and misunderstandings which heightened the tension she already felt. He seemed to have given up on her, and she on him. Where had it all gone wrong?

Another sip of red wine did not bring an answer. She looked at an old pickup truck stalled at the cross street. The driver frantically lifted the hood in the rain in an attempt to restart it. The situation in the street summed up her relationship with Ted. Would it restart?

First Love

Everyone remembers their first love affair, the one that made their heart sing. The one who stirred the passions time could not erase. It happens at different times for each of us. For me it was at secondary school. Tall, athletic, blonde, blue-eyes, vivacious, and cheerful she stole my heart completely and forever.

In contrast while at primary school I focused my attention on sports and gained a sound reputation as a skilful, competitive, and talented sportsman. My hand to eye coordination enabled me to play any sort of ball sport with ease, dexterity and poise. I captained teams, leading by example. Girls, well, they smiled at me, but my shyness prevented any interaction, except embarrassing fleeting eye contact. I did not know what to do or say to them. If they had been a ball I would have been all over them like a rash, but they were mysterious unknown creatures, objects to avoid. Nobody of my age, ten-eleven, had a girl friend, for to do so was a definite mistake, leading to being ridiculed by mates.

It all changed at secondary school. With hormones rampantly causing bodily and emotional changes my shyness grew even greater. The safest thing to do was set my sights on study, sport, and avoid attention by the girls. I tried and mostly succeeded except for one attractive girl who persisted in her quest and I could not elude. I could not easily put her out of my mind. She always seemed close by, smiling, whispering, giggling, and passing love notes and 'Milk Kisses'.

Other girls had 'crushes,' and I was <u>forced</u> to talk with them from time to time because they put me in a position where I had to respond. I felt awkward. They would send me notes saying they liked me, wanted to talk, and could we meet after school. It was difficult for me to meet anyone after school because I mostly had sports practices, or would ride my bike home alone.

Penelope, 'weaver of dreams' in Greek. I walked her home from softball practice and we kissed. On a Geography excursion requiring a bus ride I held my arm around her shoulders on the return journey. For years she carried a photograph of me in a locket around her neck. After high school I rarely saw her because our paths seldom crossed. She studied to become a teacher while I studied chemistry and geology at university. While we both caught trains from the same station for at least four years we failed to meet on the platform or in a carriage. Our meetings were not often enough to forge a relationship. She took an earlier train then stayed late to work in the library. We both played sport and therefore attended training during the week and matches on weekends. I always remember feeling she was 'the one', but I let her get away. Or did she let me?

I thought of myself as a tough kid at school, but my exploits at primary school exceeded those of everybody else. As a consequence I received regular caning by the headmaster. In the 'old' days caning was permitted to keep the boys (girls never misbehaved!), under control. It is politically incorrect these days for teachers to cane children. Later in life, I had one 'several death experiences,' but all my other troubles were minor, mostly embarrassing, although some could have been tragic if events had unfolded differently.

One day after attending primary school I was riding my bike and almost home when I saw two girls walking on the wrong side of the road. All children were taught to walk on the right hand side of the road (no footpaths) so they faced the oncoming traffic. When they saw a car coming they could step off the bitumen onto the unpaved shoulder. On this particular day my cousin, Yvonne, and her girlfriend were walking on the left hand side of the road, the same side as I was riding. Just before I overtook them they decided to change from the left hand side to the right hand side of the road. Suddenly and immediately in front of me and without looking they altered course. The inevitable happened. I had been riding fast as usual, too fast, and could not brake or swerve in time. Bam! Ouch! I collided with Yvonne and the impact sent us tumbling onto the road. Fortunately no cars were coming otherwise someone could have been killed. As I cascaded onto the bitumen I put out my right hand to break my fall, but my momentum caused me harm as I smacked hard into the road. Yvonne was slightly shocked and bruised and recovered quickly. Her main concern was the state of her clothes, a consequence of the impact. It had sent her sprawling so her dress came over her head, exposing her underpants!

Bill, a friend of mine saw what had happened because he had been riding behind me. Bill skidded to a stop and jumped off his bike. I was holding back tears as the pain from my wrist was severe. Bill dragged his bike off the road, then helped me walk to a house, where he ran cold water from a garden tap over my hand and rapidly swelling wrist. After a few minutes I stopped shaking and was able to walk home, but my wrist was swollen and hurt like hell. Bill walked both bikes to my place and explained to my mother what had happened. She ran more cold water over my wrist and then wrapped a bandage tightly on it before suspending it in a sling. The few abrasions from the fall on the road were nothing compared to the pain from the wrist. I was not able to write for a couple of days, but attended classes anyway.

I was always making trouble at school, so the Headmaster caned me regularly. I was caught talking with my friends Trevor and Robert during music class when we should have been singing. The three of us received six cane strokes on each hand. Another time I was caned for climbing through an open window of a classroom during recess to fetch a tennis ball I had thrown there. I was caned for hitting some unfortunate kid in the head with another tennis ball. Based on the kid's report I received six sharp wallops with the cane and detention at lunch and recess.

The Headmaster's punishment tool was about a metre long and the thickness of a finger, and made of a flexible bamboo cane. In his hands, an ex-league football player, it became almost a deadly weapon. He would wack it hard across the open hands, striking the finger tips so as to inflict sudden and intense pain. Obviously the corporal punishment 'message' did not travel between my fingers and my brain, because I soon making another visit for caning.

Another incident was a close call. I had my ears tugged and twisted painfully by a girl who became enraged when I pulled the wings off a butterfly. I had been walking home from school in a group when I saw a Monarch butterfly on a bush near the edge of the road. I quickly snatched at it and caught its wings between my fingers. I showed my trophy to some of the other kids and then to 'impress' one of the girls, a rather good looking one I had a crush on, I proceeded to pull the wings off. The girl flew at me like a leopard on its prey. She screamed as she tugged and twisted my ears, "How would you like your wings pulled off?"

She forced me onto the ground where I released the wingless insect. Then she thumped me as hard as she could with her fists, all the time yelling insults and abuse. Finally her sister and some of the other kids pulled her off. There was no infatuation after that event, and no chance of her ever becoming my friend. Later I wondered whether she had become a biologist or a boxer.

Another bicycle accident happened to me. The ride home from school was essentially flat. The flat sections required little exertion or effort, and I could coast along easily. The two short sections of road required hard peddling. I was almost home from school, but before reaching our front gate I needed to peddle up an incline, a slight rise in the slope of the road as it curved near the gate. On this occasion I stood up on the pedals to exert maximum weight and leverage to continue the momentum I had gained by letting the bike run down the gentle grade before reaching the slope.

Unfortunately, as I was nearing the end of the climb the chain broke and I fell heavily onto the cross bar. Apart from the shock of falling and the loss of my footing on the pedals the greatest injury was the impact of the bar on my groin. The difference in anatomy between boys and girls means any impact in that region of the body is certainly much more painful to a boy than for a girl. Tears came involuntarily to my eyes, and I stumbled to gain my balance. My feet landed on the road. I stopped dead in my tracks, trying to regain composure from the shock and pain. Pain was shooting like needles from my groin to my brain. In agony I could barely walk. However, after a few seconds to catch my breath and regain my equanimity I limped the rest of the way home, wheeling my bike. My father fixed the broken chain when he came home from work. I was sore for a day after the incident and did not let anybody know why I walked with a pained expression.

I did a similar thing another time, but not with a bike. I was playing with Terry, a friend of mine and nephew of my aunt. We had been walking across the back paddock and needed to climb a barbed wire fence to get back into the house paddock. I was the first to climb alongside a tall fence post, putting my foot on the plain wire beneath the barbed wire then lifting my other foot on top of the barb. As I was lifting my first foot up to put on the barb, the plain wire snapped and I fell onto the barbed wires with my legs straddling the wire. The barb had not broken. Because it was taut and high off the ground, my feet could not touch the ground. I was left hanging by my groin with the barb sticking me in a most delicate part of my anatomy. Terry had to help me climb off the wire. Tears were welling in my eyes as the point of the barn hit a tender nerve. It was excruciatingly painful. After we finally crossed over the fence I shuffled gingerly to my aunt's house to explain what had happened. As a nurse, my aunt insisted on inspecting the 'damage.' She found only a superficial cut in the skin. I was delighted the damage was minor until my aunt got out some antiseptic solution, tincture of iodine, and proceeded to wipe the wound. Wow! A new sensation of pain ripped through my body. It was worse than the barbed wire and the chain break put together. I screamed. Fortunately, the antiseptic treatment worked, preventing an infection. I found walking a bit difficult for a few days. Those two events almost made it impossible for me to father two beautiful daughters.

I had several encounters with snakes, where I was lucky not to have been bitten. The first was as a teenager, living in the hills. I used to walk up through the fruit trees into the paddock, hurl stones at birds, throw dry cow pats as if they were Frisbees, and just while away the time not doing much, as kids do. One warm summer day I stood studying the dry seed heads of Scotch thistle plants growing as a tall grove of weeds at the far end of a paddock. I carefully pulled the hairs from the thistle heads so I could eat the brown seeds, taking care not to get pricked by the spikes. I had been standing in the one spot for a few minutes concentrating on my task.

Only a gentle breeze blew. Cows and sheep grazed silently in the distance. I heard the seeds I accidentally dropped fall to the grass below. A rustling sound caught my ears. The noise came from close by. I turned around to look, but couldn't see anything. I heard the rustle again and looked at the ground all around, but it was difficult to see through the thistle bushes and dry brown grass. I did not move. Another rustling noise came from farther to the right. I saw it this time; a thin brown tail moving ever so slowly in my direction. It was a long brown snake with its head close to my feet.

In an instant, I leapt in the air and began running as fast as I could out of the thistle patch and towards the fruit trees and my house. Panicking, I sprinted towards the fence; my heart racing, and at break neck speed easily hurdled over the obstacle as if competing in the Olympics, thinking the snake was on my heels. An adrenalin rush surged through my body and kept me running until I approached the safety of the house. It took several minutes to calm down. The thought of a brown snake almost biting me put shivers up my spine.

The second incident was many years later during field work in Arnhem Land. I worked with Tom Waterhouse and Campbell Macgregor. My job as a geologist involved using aerial photographs to navigate to outcropping rocks, and to record their composition and position on a map. The usual practice was to leave the four-wheel drive vehicle with the driver and walk across the rocky exposure while the driver moved the vehicle to a designated meeting place on the other side of the hill. One day, I set out on my walk across a large exposure of granite, aiming to meet my driver on the other side, about 500 metres away. The rounded mound of rock was about the size of two large football fields, and about 3-5m high. I needed to cross it on foot rather than just walk around the base to get an idea of the uniformity of the composition. I angled my way towards the low summit of the mound when I saw a long brown snake heading down the rock face towards me. When we saw each other we stopped. I was close enough to see the tongue of the snake licking the air, smelling my presence. It was not a rock python, but a Taipan, one of Australia's most deadly snakes. My heart pounded with adrenalin. I did not want to move lest I provoked the snake to attack; they can be very aggressive. We eyed each other for seconds. Each of us seemed to be deciding what to do if the other one moved in their direction. I was defenceless, with no tree nearby to climb, and no stick to use for protection. My geological hammer would be an inappropriate weapon against a rapidly advancing agile snake.

At the same instant as I slowly edged my left foot to the left the snake slid its head to its left. Cautiously I moved farther to my left. The snake did the same. We gradually crept farther apart. In a flash, the snake slid off. If it had decided to strike and bite me, I would have been dead before my driver came to look for me.

Another episode as a kid taught me a lesson. I must have been about ten years old when I almost lost the top of the index finger on my left hand. I was experimenting again, this time trying to make a dart or short arrow. I had taken a piece of wood from the side of a broken half-case used for fruit and had cut it into a long shaft about the thickness of my finger. My Dad used a knife to cut leather for repairing our shoes and its edge was razor sharp. Just the tool I needed for cutting a point on my dart. I had cut two slots in the tail section and had also cut out two pieces of thin cardboard from an empty shirt carton to make the tail 'feathers.' The last chore was to cut a point and to carefully make notches around the shaft in front of the tail feathers so I could tie a piece of knotted string for the 'woomera' or lever to help me propel the dart.

It was almost lunch time and my Mum had called me. I hurried to finish my task when the knife slipped and deeply cut into my index finger. The top of my finger was hanging by the skin. I had cut through the nail and exposed the bone. The pain was excruciatingly severe, but I managed to manipulate the finger tip back into its position on the bloodied cut surface and hold it firmly in place with my thumb. It throbbed like nothing I had felt before, and blood ran everywhere. I took the knife and dart back to the shed, went to the bathroom and fixed two band-aids to hold the tip of my finger in place. I swallowed two pain killers, and walked nonchalantly into the kitchen to eat my lunch. The wound healed and the nail grew back on my finger.

Another time I almost killed himself was driving home from a party when I momentarily fell asleep at the wheel. Kerry, a tall brunette laboratory assistant from Western Australia, and I had driven to a party at a friend's place. The girl lived in the country outside of Canberra, and we drove there one Saturday night for dinner and drinks. I had met Kerry at the Government Hostel where we resided. We were 'going steady.' The night in question was another 'date.'

The party continued until after midnight when we said farewell and headed back to the hostel. I had consumed two or three beers over several hours, and while not drunk was suffering fatigue after the long week at work. It was also well after my usual bed time. I drove an orange-brown Ford. Kerry dozed. About half-way back to Canberra along a straight stretch of road, on the Yass side of the village of Hall, I suddenly heard bumpy bump bump. It was the sound of the tyres running over the rough edge of the road, but on the wrong side. Fortunately, no other cars were travelling the road at the time. Waking instantly I steered back to the left hand side, and slowed the car. Gently shaking Kerry on the shoulder to wake her up I explained what had happened and instructed her to talk to me until we reached the hostel.

The next near death experience was almost being killed in the Northern Territory in the last year of the field campaign of geological mapping. A drilling crew was testing the subsurface geology across a geological formation called the Nanambu Complex, near the South Alligator River, and it was my turn as one of three geologists to spend a week with the drilling team. My role was to log the cuttings coming up the bore hole. I had been in

Darwin with John (my driver) spending a weekend to relax after several weeks of field work near the East Alligator River.

John had previously owned a grocery shop in England, and one day decided to sell it, buy a bicycle and ride to Australia. He took his bike across the channel by ferry and then rode to Singapore where he sold it to buy a ferry ticket to sail through Indonesia to Darwin. The geological party leader hired John as a cook and alternate driver for our field campaign. John needed to take driving lessons in Darwin before he could apply for the job because he had never driven a car, let alone a vehicle off-road and through the bush. To say John was inexperienced as a driver, especially in Australian outback conditions, was a gross understatement. A prior experience with John was when he had run off a dirt road and almost collided with a tree. He said he lost control of the steering wheel while trying to drive and simultaneously roll a cigarette. I told me after the incident he just shut his eyes and hoped not to hit anything. Fortunately the car stalled before we hit a tree.

The near death episode occurred after John was handed keys to a brand spanking new, yellow, long-wheel base four-wheel drive Toyota in Darwin. He proudly drove with me as passenger south from Darwin, turned off the Stuart Highway and headed out on the bitumen road towards the South Alligator River. Road crews using heavy equipment were upgrading the road from dirt to bitumen, making the journey to the Jabiru Uranium camp about a two hour drive and not a dusty eight hour trip as in the past. Two kilometres west of the South Alligator River crossing John took a turn onto a single vehicle track leading north towards the location of the drillers. It was a reasonably good track because it provided access for many vehicles going to Munmalary Homestead, a buffalo and cattle property.

John and I stopped soon after the turn off to relieve their bladders, and then we headed off again. Being a hot day we did not reconnect our seat belts because we intended driving at moderate speed and were unlikely to meet cars coming the other way. John talked about his bicycle adventures as we sped along a flat stretch of straight road. As with all bush tracks the straight stretches end in bends and John, focused intently on the details of his bicycle adventures, forgot how fast we travelled. The road turned sharply at the end of the straight stretch and John maintained the speed of the car despite warnings from me. John did not expect such a sharp deviation in the direction of the track and lost control., while attempting to maintain the speed and steer so the tyres remained in the two worn tracks. The back wheels slid out of the ruts onto the sandy verge causing the vehicle to skid sideways. John kept his foot on the accelerator propelling the car forward. The back end of the vehicle hit a tree that was growing near the rutted track. Bam! My door flew open on impact. Because I was not wearing a seat belt the momentum of the collision carried my upper body out through the open door. Fortunately for me I had wound the window down and I clutched desperately onto the door and open window frame. My legs were dragging on the floor of the car. With most of my weight hanging precariously outside the door I could not pull myself back inside the cabin. From the dangling position I looked along the side of the car and quickly realised where the vehicle was headed; towards three robust trees lining the edge of the track, right in the path of the speeding vehicle. Meanwhile, oblivious to what was happening to his passenger, John kept the accelerator to the floor and kept talking.

Three trees loomed large and in direct line with me and the side of the car. Recognising the danger I faced I instantly released my grip and fell out of the car. On hitting the ground I heard an almighty 'Bam!' My open door had crashed hard against the first tree and slammed shut. The momentum of the vehicle and my weight carried me forward along the dirt road for a few metres before I came to a dusty painful stop. John kept on driving for another few hundred metres before he turned to see I was missing. After the car had scraped the second tree, John said he turned to look at me to say "that was close!" But my seat was empty.

Winded, sore and dusty I tried standing, but could not. A sharp pain wracked my left rib cage on which I had landed. I could only take shallow breaths as my ribs 'hurt like hell,' Dirt stuck in my mouth and dust covered my body. Dark red blood oozed though my torn shirt from the abrasions. Blood also ran from scratches and abrasions on my legs. Dirt filled one eye making sight temporarily impossible.

John had stopped the vehicle and walked back to where I was assessing my injuries, but he did not bring any water or medical kit. Seeing my abrasions and bloody condition John raced back to the car and brought a bottle of water. I washed my face, eyes and scratches. I still couldn't breathe properly; only painfully sucking in small mouthfuls of air. My side hurt and my body ached. Panicking, John ripped the shirt off my back to inspect the wounds thinking I was severely injured. The shirt was tattered, dirty and blood stained and he needed to look at it quickly so he could wash the dirt out of the bloody abrasions.

We then took stock of our position. It was a long drive back to Darwin. I was hurt, but OK, and could survive. There did not appear to be any broken bones. We decided to drive to Munmalary Station and get some first aid there from the property owner, before heading to the drilling site.

The wife of the property owner found some antiseptic liquid and washed the abrasions. She also washed most of the dirt and dust from my body, face and hair before making tea and serving biscuits. John rang the Darwin office to tell them I had been in an accident, but was only slightly injured and would stay to work at the drilling site.

It was a painful ride to the drilling site because I felt every jarring bump. Each jolt caused a sharp pain as if I had cracked my ribs. My rib cage remained painful for months. I could not sleep on my left side, but tolerated the constant pain and stayed for the week at the drill site working as if nothing had happened. I did not receive any sympathy from the drillers. They just kidded John about his driving ability and he was just another Pommy Bastard who was not good enough to kill a geologist!

It was not the end of the story. After the car had hit the tree John and I only superficially examined the four-wheel drive. It looked as if the damage was confined to a few scratches down the left hand side and one indentation where the rear end had collided with the first tree. We were wrong. On our way back to Darwin at the end of the week we were passed by a car the driver of which had kept honking his car horn and flashing his lights, indicating for us to stop. We stepped out of the car to see the problem the other driver had seen. The back axle was glowing red hot. The oil in the axle case had drained out through a small fracture caused by the impact with the tree. As there was no lubricant in the axle, metal had been rubbing against metal generating extreme heat. John and I waited for the axle to cool down, then we removed the axle shaft. By putting the vehicle into four wheel drive we were able to continue our laborious journey back to Darwin using front wheel drive only.

The mechanic in Darwin explained the collision with the tree had bent the car's chassis slightly out of alignment and the vehicle was a write-off. It was a one trip vehicle. The bureaucratic paperwork was mountainous for the vehicle and for me. An X-ray in the hospital revealed I did not have any broken ribs and a full medical check up indicated I was fine.

The next incident occurred when I visited a colleague at Rum Jungle, south of Darwin. My mate was re-mapping the rocks of the uranium area around Rum Jungle. After a day in the field examining various rock exposures and talking about the geology of the area we went to the local club to eat dinner, drink beer and play pool. It was nearing closing time when we left the club. I walked outside first while my mate said farewell to several of his friends. Whack! The next instant I was lying on my back on the ground. I had been king-hit.

According to my mate who saw the incident an Aboriginal guy who had been in the club had followed me out of the club. As I turned around the Aboriginal guy hit me square on the chin with his fist. Of course I did not know the blow was coming. All I saw was a pair of eyes up close. The next instant I was on the ground, stunned. Why I received the blow remained a mystery. The skin on my jaw was broken in a cut about 1 cm long, and blood oozed out. My mate advised me to leave town. With a band-aid across the wound I drove back to Darwin. There was no arrest for the assault and I never found out who hit me. I only heard later about a white fella being king-hit by a black guy, and everything was OK. The wound healed up, but the scar remained.

A second and longer scar later joined the one from the king-hit. I almost lost several teeth, but fortunately, and by good chance my handsome looks were preserved. In Canberra, I played cricket for two clubs; City and Ginninderra. I was playing for City against North and they batted first. We had lost several wickets when it was my turn to bat. I had not made many runs and was facing Geoff 'Chucka' Clark. Chucka Clarkie was well known in Canberra because his bowling action was suspect, and instead of delivering a ball in a round bowling action he occasionally surprised batsmen by illegally throwing the ball at great speed. Surprise was the word because the speed of the thrown delivery was at least twice as fast as his normal bowling pace. On this day Chucka was using a short run up and bowling medium-paced deliveries. He threw a fast ball. It pitched short and rose up sharply. I quickly tried to get into position to play a pull shot, but the ball was so much faster than I had expected. Before I could get my bat around to hit the ball, the ball had careered into my chin. Whack!

Blood flowed from a wide deep gash. I was advised by the surrounding players, who had rushed up to see what had happened, to go to the hospital for stitches. One of the players' wives took me to Canberra Hospital, which was then located on the site of the current National Museum. I waited for a short time in emergency and then was attended to by a doctor who put 23 stitches in my chin. He also gave me a tetanus injection, and a pain killer. I went back to the game, but did not return to the field.

About a week later I went to the outpatients department of the hospital where two nurses had great fun pulling out the stitches. It was fun for them, but not for me because I had not been able to shave around the wound and my dark whiskers looked like the black stitching thread. Occasionally a nurse pulled on a hair and not the stitch. Ouch!! They laughed. Ouch!. I was lucky the ball did not hit me square in the mouth and knock out my teeth. Keep your eye on the ball next time!!

The next near death experience came after returning to Adelaide from a trip to the USA. In July 2018 I landed at Adelaide airport and noticed I was suffering from shortness of breath. I thought I had picked up a 'bug' on the plane and simply required antibiotics. I made a booking at the General Practitioner's for the next day. I slept well. In the morning and breathing easier I considered cancelling my appointment. I changed my mind when I remembered I had not received the results of the previous blood test. At nine o'clock I entered the GP's rooms. Dr John Varona had been my GP for several years. I explained what my symptoms were. He listened to my breathing and heart, then said for me to follow him. He wanted to conduct an ECG (electrocardiogram). I was perplexed and said something like, 'Why do you want to do it. It's only a chest infection?"

"Follow me!"

I did. He and the nurse hovered around me like he had never done before. Something is not right, I thought. Impatiently the Doctor waited for the scan to print.

"I'll give you fifteen minutes to get to Emergency,' he announced emphatically. 'Is there anybody who can drive you or shall I call an ambulance?"

"What?"

"You're in AF, atrial fibrillation and your lungs are blocked. You need specialist care. Immediately!"

I rang my sister. She drove my to Flinders Medical where I was admitted. An X-ray of my chest indicated 60% loss of function. My heart rate was well over a hundred. I was given Amiodarone to take and required to inject Clexane as a blood thinner. I also needed to take Ramipril and Bisoprolol. Gradually the clots in my lungs dissolved and I received the first of five cardioversions (jump starts) to bring my heart into rhythm. Later, 6 June 2021 and as a consequence of taking Amiodarone I experienced a thyroid shock. I spent three nights in hospital while Dr Stephen Hedger diagnosed an overactive thyroid. I was taken off Amiodarone and put on Carbimazole and Prednisolone. By controlling my medication doses for an overactive thyroid and using regular blood tests I was able to return my thyroid hormones (T3, T4) to normal levels. I now only take blood thinning medication to lower the risk of blood clots.

Mongolian experiences

Wednesday 30 June, 2010, Ulaanbaatar (UB).

The morning was cold, cloudless and a keen wind blew clouds of dust. After checking our bags at the desk we drank tea while we waited for security checks and boarding our ageing Fokker 50 (twin propeller) Aero Mongolian flight. Queue jumping is an art form and essentially achieved by getting a colleague or friend to slip to the counter on one side while the anxious traveller deposits their bags near the balance on the other side of the line. The friend accosts the attendant and pushes the ticket forward, encouraging action while the traveller lifts their bags casually onto the scale as soon as the previous bags have been tagged and moved. Done simply without fuss and few people notice, just impatient westerners keen to vacate the line and take their flight.

The flight to Ölgii (see map) was generally smooth except for a short period of turbulence encountered when passing billowing clouds near thunderheads and then on descent to a dirt runway to the north of a town flanking a green corridor adjacent to a twisting river. Bags were unloaded by Kazakhs, hard faced and brown, onto a cart towed by a slow moving tractor which bumped to a concrete pad near the terminal entrance. As this was occurring the passengers, waiting to fly back to UB, walked across the tarmac to the plane for their three-hour flight to civilisation. A porter checked the tags on each bag against the ticket before allowing entrance into the terminal. Toilet facilities exist outside the terminal. Near the car park stands a wooden structure covering a long foul smelling trench. Planks line the trench enabling a comfortable squat. Welcome to western Mongolia!

Matthew, my boss and I were met in Ölgii by Jerry (geologist) and his driver Armac from Gobi Coal and Energy and Dashkar (our driver) and Sirchin a retired geologist working part-time for Origino (our company). I joined Jerry in his vehicle while Matthew went with Dashkar and Sirchin. We headed out of town travelling south along a thin bitumen road for a mile and then drove onto a gravel ungraded road.

Brown mountains stood naked and roughly on each side of a narrow valley with gradual slopes up to a low pass on the left hand side. The range became capped by snow and we followed it for many kilometres. The rugged right side had patches of snow but was mostly green, formed in sweeping carpet like grass and wildflowers.

The first thing I noticed was the purity of the air and the consequential deceptiveness of distance perspective. Mountains appeared close, but were a long way off. Landmarks seeming near took many minutes to reach even at 80 km/hr. The landscape captured the eye and presented a paradise for photographer and painter. Broad valleys curved upwards to brown craggy ridges and narrow peaks. White snow capped distant mountains and lower, jagged and contorted ranges skirted the middle distance above long blue lakes. Clusters of white gers dotted the landscape around which brown and white flocks of sheep and goats grazed. Thin cattle roamed the unfenced terrain.

After a bumpy and dusty hour, we arrived at a Soum, a village comprising brick and mortar house and iron buildings on a wide green grassy flat beneath towering mountains. There we waited for our guide to show us to the camp called Ulaan Ghajuu, a copper exploration site. A thin track snaked through the grassy lowland between gers and dark skinned locals who were attending to chores and herding their animals. The dusty track gradually climbed up a long valley to a boulder-strewn slope, then on to a steep rocky crest and to a pass, just below snowline. The vehicle crawled towards a wide green valley and then sped recklessly down a brown treeless slope to a green pasture where white gers and flocks dotted the scene. Eventually we wound around and through rocks to a cluster of three gers erected at the bottom of a valley – our temporary home.

Meals were based on a watery soup containing mutton and pasta. Homemade sweet bread was spread with jam or the equivalent of Nutella and washed down with black tea or milk tea (from various animals – horse, goat, sheep). No vegetables or fruit! A young woman with round beaming face in her early twenties happily prepared our meals, boiled water for tea and heated milk. She made bread every second day. The table where we ate had small bowls of wrapped sweets and caramels. Lumps of dried yogurt and boiled milk residue were available, but I found them strongly flavoured and unpalatable.

Five of us slept in the same ger. The cook had her own bed ornately decorated with blue patterned fabric awnings. It was decorated with tassels, mirrors and a few small ornaments. Earplugs reduced the sound of snoring and I had one of my best sleeps in weeks. Matthew and I had bought sleeping bags and were glad we did because the cold mountain air had a crisp chill.

Disappointed with the copper project we left the next day and drove back to Ölgii so Matthew and Sirchin could fly to UB. We stayed in a Russian-built hotel where the toilet, shower and plumbing had not been maintained and were useless. What can one expect for 18000 Tugrik (US$14/night).

Brown and yellow-brown hawks scavenged for food scraps out the back of the hotel. They circled above the town and dropped in a controlled descent onto ladders and scaffolding being used for exterior repairs. Small brown and white finches and black ravens shared the air space. No jet trails or sound of planes except the once daily flight to and from UB.

At 7am the next morning and without breakfast we headed to our next camp, Red Hill. Jerry and his driver led the way in the 2008 Toyota Land cruiser belonging to Gobi Coal and Energy. Dashkar and I followed in his personal 1997 Land cruiser. We quickly traversed the same section of road as we had travelled the previous days before we commenced the remainder of an arduous 15 hour trek.

The unmade track followed valley floors as it was the easiest route. On the flat open plain we easily sped at 90-100km/hr. These flat stretches gave way to slopes and rocky passes where we crawled at 10km/hr over rough ground. Each saddle had a large pile of rocks decorated with blue cloth or flags on wooden poles fluttering in the wind. We stopped at several so Jerry's driver could circle them on foot and add stones – a Buddhist ritual. By lunch we had arrived at Hovd and after eating our first meal of the day we refuelled and headed through the backbone of Mongolian geology – a rugged range cut by fast flowing streams shedding from the snow capped mountains.

The start of this section was over flat terrain, and we followed a long narrow valley for an hour at high speed, only slowing were the occasional large rock or hollow made us swerve. The choice of track on which to drive was an individual thing because roads do not exist and many single vehicle tracks run in the general direction. Most used tracks have many corrugations and it is easier to make a new track or follow one with fewer closely spaced troughs. A series of undulating and twisting river crossings announced the end of the section and heralded the start of slower driving across the shallow network of braided channels. Gaining the opposite side at last we veered south and took a track leading upwards along another valley floor to the start of a six-hour torturous route through narrow mountain passes and rough ground. Families and villages tranquilly occupied the green fertile valley bottoms near fast-flowing streams, winding their way serpentine-like to distant lakes. Sheep, cattle, yaks, goats and camels grazed on the green pasture.

A nomadic family was on the move, their camels loaded with folded gers and possessions. Two women leisurely led two rows of packed camels while their husbands rode horses and trailed spare ones on ropes. Slow but steady progress they made unlike our motorised hurtle down long slopes and bone crunching crawls over rocky tracks and rough stream crossings. On each side of the track tall mountain ridges embraced our view and constrained our route. Then, wide green valleys opened up as the ranges spread out, allowing clusters of gers and nomadic families' space to live and survive, perpetuating a culture long lost in UB. Each ger had one heap of flattened dung piled high as a fuel for domestic fires. Few trees grew along the stream banks and coal was scarce. Low technology was obvious in these remote parts and garages and repair shops were nonexistent. The track we travelled ran close to dwellings which surprised the eye. Satellite dishes, solar panels and flat screen TV sets abounded, contrasting to the appearance of simplicity of a nomadic existence.

Twice we stopped in fifteen hours to spell the drivers, urinate, eat and drink. These short stops were the only breaks we took because our focus was to reach the next camp before dark. There were no hotels along the route, and no restaurants or snack bars. Finally, we emerged from the ruggedness and twisting mountain ravine and emerged onto a vast brown plain where in the distance we could see a Soum where we refuelled. An irrigation ditch caused navigation problems and signposts did not point us where we needed to go. Locals waved their arms and yelled instructions and finally we headed southwest along one of many tracks. At a saddle, the tracks diverged and initially Dashkar drove to the right only to spot the distant cloud of dust from Jerry's vehicle heading left towards a construction site. A short while later we climbed an embankment to the black bitumen of the China road; being built by Chinese labourers so trucks heavy with coal could feed China's enormous resource appetite.

Typical Mongolian Highway.

We sped past transports loaded with steel for road construction and raced towards the mountain range we just crossed. At a village, near the entrance to a canyon, we branched east and followed tracks along creek beds and over rocks, through fields of red and yellow wildflowers. We were tired and the drivers exhausted but we were nearly at our destination. The yellow light from the setting sun cast long shadows and distorted the landscape.

In the distance and with the sun low, the soft yellow light losing power we finally saw Red Hill, a reddish peak of rock protruding from a narrow plain between two bare rocky mountain ranges. Thirty minutes later, at 10pm and just as a world cup soccer game was about to start (and be seen in a ger fitted with satellite dish and TV) we parked in the designated area at the camp: three gers aligned so their doorways faced east.

Sumiya, the young geologist in charge and his crew greeted us hastily so they could return to watching Holland play Brazil. The crew included Choi, a geology student, Kulan, the cook, and her assistant Ganana. Kulan knew we were coming and had prepared a meal of mutton and pasta stew which we hungrily consumed.

Exhausted we found our beds in a ger: wooden platforms made by Ganana. Though hard at first the beds felt comfortable and we slept soundly while the football game played out. The early sunrise woke me. Understandably, the drivers slept until 10am and by then I had walked around Red Hill and made observations about the previous drilling sites and possible future locations to test the gold-bearing rocks.

Rock pigeons visited the camp. They have dark grey heads, pale grey bodies and white and dark bars on their tail feathers. An iridescent neck seemed to distinguish the sexes. Small finches sang, but are difficult to see. A golden breasted duck inhabited wet areas near the river. Mosquitoes were abundant at the camp and to pass the time while sitting we slapped and clapped to kill them. Small black flies were also common, but of nuisance value. The open pit toilet attracted larger flies in droves and as the weak slats gave me cause for concern I only used it once before I found a sandy creek bed 500m away.

While waiting for the rig to arrive from UB we visited sites, talked and read. I spent time memorising Mongolian numbers, days of the week and other common words. I read and thought, and reflected on being there. I thought about what to do and how to proceed on this and other projects. I knew soon all would be busy because the core will need logging, examining and selecting for assaying. Decisions with severe financial implications depended on the outcome of the first few diamond drill holes.

Monday 5th July.

Each day four or five pigeons would land in front of the kitchen ger and peck for food scraps. Kulan would throw waste water with particles of food out for them. One pigeon had a limp. Its left foot was curled, so it walked gingerly around pecking at the ground.

I ran out of pens and pencils writing notes and was given a new pen by Sumiya. I am prompted to write about our ger in which I sleep because of a major improvement in my personal circumstances; a mattress. After arriving at the Red Hill camp I slept for seven nights in a sleeping bag directly on top of wooden planks nailed to make a bed. With the comfort of a 6" mattress my hips have rejoiced even though they had adjusted to the unevenness of the boards. I soon learnt the position of the uneven board and could control rolling over so I stayed within the limits of the board.

Actually, I slept very well. The sun was setting late, about 10pm and rising early, about 5 am and I usually saw both.

Our ger like every ger I imagine is circular about 6m in diameter and domed to about 3m at the round circular vent and is 1.3m wide at the apex of the ceiling/roof. The roof is supported by 70 straight wooden poles attached to the apex frame and the outer wall support. The entrance faces east and stands 1.3m high. It has a door opening outwards and a stoop or step about a foot high. The frame of the doorway is made of wood and after hitting my head twice I quickly remembered to bend my head first before stepping across the threshold rather than the other way around. Ouch!

There are no windows because the walls are framed in wooden slats nailed in a crisscross fashion. The outside layer is made of felt (like under carpet used to be, if you are old enough to remember under carpet). The felt layer is about 2cm thick and then a white canvas encloses the entire structure, except for a flap at the opening at the apex of the roof. Skilfully manoeuvring a rope enables the flap of canvas to be pulled across the opening; useful during rain or snow. The central hole serves as an air vent when it is hot and for access to a chimney pipe which runs up from the back of the rectangular stove.

Men erecting a ger at the exploration camp.

For 'air conditioning' in hot weather the felt skirt is lifted around the side of the ger where the wind is blowing and the ceiling flap opened. During rain the skirt is dropped and the roof flap closed.

Essentially the problem with the drilling program was the antiquity of the equipment. The water tanker was more than 30 years old, the drill rig was at least 20 years old, our car was a 1997 Toyota and I worried it would fail on the return journey to UB. One of the two spare tyres was already shredded. Exploration demands new equipment, regular maintenance and well-trained staff, but Mongolia lacks these essential elements. I wondered how the equity investment strategy would turn out.

Waiting for the drilling rig to arrive at Red Hill tested everybody's patience. It was supposed to arrive on Sunday, but by the following Wednesday evening we were told it may arrive the following day. To pass the time I worked with the geologist and his assistant on various small projects. We walked along a rocky ridge and climbed 300m to a cliff while inspecting the alteration of the rocks and the traces of copper in fractures.

I borrowed a dictionary and refreshed my memory of the Cyrillic alphabet and noted numbers, colours and selected Mongolian phrases I intended to use frequently, as well as mineral names.

I read "The Women" by T. C. Boyle, a book about the three wives of Frank Lloyd Wright. I also began making notes for my new novel on scraps of paper I scrounged. I thought up a title to reflect the struggle of my main character, Jane Bell (my great great grandmother from Ireland). I tentatively called the book "Uphill across the sea." I think it fitted with an Irish theme for the book...don't you think? I might change it to "Another tide in the sea" to reflect the repetitive highs and lows of the tide of 'fortunes' in her life.

On Tuesday night the wind blew steadily, a blessing because the mosquitoes were not airborne. We awoke Wednesday to an overcast sky and a few droplets of rain. After breakfast at 8am, which consisted of bread, jam and coffee, the rain began and continued steadily all day. It was a soft gentle rain. I finished reading my book and then lay on my sleeping bag, wrote, reflected and did anything to distract me from thinking about all the reports accumulating in

UB and awaiting my review. Not only work, but I needed to choose an apartment, buy groceries and establish a productive routine. The rain was a blessing because the parched desert surely needed invigorating. I guessed the mosquitoes wiould be back in abundance when the sun resumed its daily arc without the dark blanket of clouds hovering over us.

The brown ground turned darker with the rain, but puddles did not form because the desiccated sponge of rock and gravel absorbed every drop, sucking it deep into the parched earth. Small shallot-like plants and a pincushion ground cover with short tufts of feathery grass drank up the moisture with green delight. All activities stopped during the rain. Birds did not fly; insects stopped buzzing, lizards hid under rocks and the wind retired.

The rain eased off for a while enabling me to walk around the nearby hills behind the camp. A brown hawk circled silently on a spiral path, rising effortlessly in search of prey. Two ravens cawed in the distance. Several types of finch flew low to the ground; one I call a flap-tail because of its idiosyncratic behaviour. A solitary swift or swallow coasted acrobatically above the camp catching mosquitoes.

Our camp of three gers was located on a gentle slope that ran down from a rocky series of black and brown ridges. The three white gers formed circles in a northerly row all with entrances facing east. They stood out starkly in the landscape barren of trees. We looked eastward to another camp where the drillers were living. There was no order there, the gers were scattered between dumps of supplies, equipment and trucks. Beyond the drillers' camp was a yellow brown hill, a pinnacle remnant from an explosive neck that once shook the earth in majestic eruptions many millions of years ago.

Blue skies developed thin streaky cirrus clouds. They evaporated or formed into fluffy cumulus shapes even as I watched. They constantly changed and disappeared. In the distance tall, white and dark cumulo-nimbus clouds hovered over mountain ranges. A grey mist and remnant rain veiled the nearby hills as the rain steadily fell. Too much rain now and the heavy drilling rig would slip and slide, and probably bog down in the sodden clay pans – just what we don't need! At 3.30pm the rain stopped. Seven hours of steady moisture; tranquillity over powering all senses.

Kulan (her name means wild horse), the cook was about 168cm tall. I estimated she was in her late twenties, thin and slightly bent over with hunched shoulders. Her thin face hid behind wide spectacles and her grey eyes flashed and sparkled hinting at sharp intelligence. Her long brown hair formed a well-tied single plait. It fell to the small of her back. Neat white teeth shone through a wide smile greeting me every time we met. Small dark brown moles speckled her face, a larger one near the corner of her mouth attracted the eye. While not speaking English she understood 'byhitler,' my way of trying to say 'thank you' in Mongolian after each meal.

Despite the heat of summer Kulan cooked on a wood stove set in the middle of the ger. The fire raged in a rectangular metal box with an opening hatch at the front for adding fuel and stoking. A large round hole on the top surface provided access for wide woks to heat. A thin long pipe ran upwards out the back of the box to carry smoke out the central vent in the roof. In winter and during the cooling rain the cooking fire added warmth to the ger, but with the sun blazing down she asked people to lift the side wall flaps so fresh air ventilated the space. Any wind was favourable, but it came in gusts stirring dust, but keeping the mosquitoes grounded, albeit temporarily.

Kulan wore a knitted off-white blouse with a thin lace border around the high V neckline, at the base of which was a pink floral decoration. A drawstring around the waist kept the blouse tight around her slender midriff and added emphasis to her small breasts. She wore dark blue tracksuit pants and pale blue plastic sandals decorated with a small solitary sunflower ornament near the big toe. Kulan's small nose on a large round face supported glasses. Perched precariously near the end was the small rise supporting the frame. I feared they would topple into the cooking pot when she lowered her head to stir the boiling mass. But hooked behind large ears the frames kept the glasses firmly in place. She wore no jewellery, no makeup or nail polish – plain! Her hands were strong with long broad fingers, almost like a man's hand.

Bread making happened every other day. Kulan used the flour we had brought and mixed other ingredients she had to make the dough. After kneading the dough she placed it in a dish near the fire and later cooked it on the fire, turning the flat ellipsoid when half was cooked. The flattened football-shaped bread was cut into slices to eat with either jam, Nutella or butter, and enjoyed with tea or soup.

Meal times were noisy. Imagine four young men slurping their watery meal of lamb chunks with noodles and a few chopped potatoes floating in a greasy fluid. The soup resembled washing water after the dishes have been cleaned. The men slurped repeatedly and heartily leaving nothing to the imagination about their hunger. There were three types of slurp: short, long and a double slurp. It all depended on what the spoon collected. If only liquid then a short slurp sucked up the fluid. A long slurp where liquid and a lump of meat or pasta were present, and a double slurp where several different foodstuffs were on the spoon. With good western manners I rarely slurped, sluuuurped or sluu-sluuurped. As guest of honour I was served first and often finished eating before the others were served. Sometimes my meal came and then the others ate shortly after. In those occasions I finish last such was the hunger of the men.

Ganana is the assistant cook and 'partner' of Kulan. He is subordinate to Kulan in the kitchen, but does lots of tasks many of which virtually go unnoticed. Sumiya is the young geologist. At 27 years old he runs the geological field work. He is married and they have a daughter, 3 years old. When in UB they share an apartment on the south side of town and pay $10/month. Some apartment compared to mine!! Some salary! He stands 183cm tall, has a slender build, dark hair cut short like most Mongolian men. He smokes, likes sleeping in late. He translates for me and his English is of a medium standard, meaning his vocabulary is not very extensive. Without his help though I would be playing charades and waving my arms frantically in efforts to convey meaning. Choi, the other geologist, has a shortened name typical of Mongolian names. He is a student of geology in his second year. He stands more than 183 cm tall and is a lanky thin youth with an awkward gawkiness. His English is as good as my Mongolian!

We are waiting for the water tanker to arrive back in camp. The engine failed and a replacement from another truck was being fitted. Without water we cannot drill because water cools the bit and removes the cuttings. To obtain diesel fuel the tanker trailer was driven 150km to a Soum where it broke down. It is an old Russian-made truck, having the reputation for lasting a long time, but also failing dramatically.

Back to waiting, sleeping, writing and reading. Just when I thought my environment had improved with the supply of a mattress brought by the drilling crew and their supplies I was confronted with a greater upgrade requiring tact and diplomacy. An envoy of the company owner, his nephew Bajig, arrived in camp and insisted I change gers to a better one – the one where Sumiya and Choi were sleeping. I did not see why it was necessary to relocate because I liked the new 'home' and had grown accustomed to its idiosyncrasies of noise and airflow. More confronting was the insistence by Bajig I change my bed from the on-site wood and nail construction to a new, fancily carved and machine made bed (probably Chinese) with head frame and structure supported by bolts. After consulting Sumiya I consented to replacing my old bed for the luxury new one, primarily to save their embarrassment. However, I firmly insisted we not change gers. In keeping with the upgrade Dashkar had his plank bed replaced as well.

Along with the new bed came a large Esky filled with broccoli that was 3-days old and kept unrefrigerated or without ice (phew!). There was also cheese, eggs, packaged sausage, cucumbers, juice and three tins of baked beans (not fresh green beans as I had requested – oh well!!). I was presented with the Esky, so I instructed the drillers to take it to Kulan so she could use the food for everyone, not just me. I kept some orange juice which I shared with Dashkar

Saturday 10 July.

The Naadam Festival started today throughout Mongolia. It is a period of four days of games and public holiday during which contests are held in wrestling, horse riding and archery. Today two events marked our day: the non-arrival of the water truck and the slaughtering of a sheep. A truck from the Soum where the water tanker had broken down towed the diesel wagon trailer into camp with news the engine of the water truck had not been replaced and would not be until after Tuesday, when Naadam had finished.

Ganana, the drilling supervisor decided to adopt my suggestion of the previous day and use the small water tank trailer to haul water to the drilling rig and fill the tanks so drilling could start. The small tank only holds 2000 litres and the tank on the drilling rig requires at least 7500 litres. Throughout the day they hauled water and the drillers organised their gear so they could begin to drill. At 8pm the rig started turning, finally!

Two brown hawks with pale white bars on their wings soared effortlessly around the area all afternoon. Four ravens cawed their way westward. Three finches chirped as they flew low to the ground in a stuttered flight pattern. One black beetle crawled from under a small bush and ventured between the rocks. Dashkar found a second large spider and captured it in a glass jar. Three gecko-like lizards scurried across my path as I walked around the low hills north of the camp in a sweep of the terrain looking at rocks, and trying to find ancient artefacts, but without luck. A small piece of obsidian of nondescript shape is the only evidence (apart from piles of rocks) of previous inhabitants of this area.

Unlike all other locations, perhaps excluding Mexico, the drillers do not bring already assembled core trays, but make them on site from plywood, wooden slats and nails. They fasten the rectangular plywood sheet at each end with slats, then run narrow slats between the ends to form a series of rows or troughs to hold the core. The slats are nailed through the plywood and at each end, making a sturdy tray. The first of the core trays should soon be used because core will be pulled from the first few metres of drilling.

My left knee, the 'good' one is still giving me intense pain, particularly when moving into a standing position from a squat. It's certainly better than a week ago when most movement gave constant pain. Why it is giving me hell I can't explain – maybe gout or old age! The right knee, which usually slips out and gives me concern because of weak ligaments, is fine – touch wood. Initially, I thought I must have positioned it badly during one of my flights, but there seems to be a more serious problem or more severe damage to ligaments than I had thought. Walking is fine except the jarring impacts going downhill when excruciating pain almost forces me to stop. After sitting for a while, I need to stretch it because the ache begins and continues unrelenting. Almost two weeks and the problem persists, although reduced in intensity.

Mild weather continued. While the days were warm they are not excessively hot and at night the clear skies release heat from the earth making for ideal sleeping conditions. The stars seem so close because the air is clear and there is no radiated light from civilisation to weaken the intensity of each star or Milky Way. The moon has waned to a slip of a crescent, but the starlight is bright enough to see without a torch. Clouds build during the day and then dissipate. Thin cirrus clouds are common. No aeroplanes pass overhead. No ants crawl. Deer flies (March flies) are abundant, taking over from the mosquitoes.

I find it interesting how we can take an instant liking or disliking to someone the first time we meet them? With Sumiya I felt an instant liking, but his cousin, Bajig was the opposite. Sumiya retreated into himself and lost confidence. Bajig swaggered arrogantly into the ger and immediately barked orders at Dashkar who was perplexed, and rightly so because Dashkar did not work for Bajig. Dashkar works for Origino and is my driver whereas

Bajig works for Universal Minerals. Nevertheless, Dashkar jumped to comply with the orders. The orders were to leave the ger and move to the other one where Sumiya was living. Apparently he was trying to impress me by giving me a better ger. When I politely refused by saying I was "mash san" (very happy) to stay where I was he then verbally attacked Sumiya, demanding he influence me to change my mind. I consented to changing beds, but not moving and this placated Bajig to some extent.

Later, around camp Bajig barked orders and everyone jumped to obey. He would strut around the kitchen demanding Kulan immediately make him something to eat – before she had served others who were waiting. He would push chairs out of the way brusquely and forcefully move things about on the table. He shouted rather than talked. He yelled at the female geologist, Gerle, who had accompanied him to the field from UB.

"Bring me water so I can wash my hands," he commanded.

Everyone else fetched their own water. In contrast, Sumiya is gentle, civil and kind. He is slightly reticent because he lacks confidence speaking English but he never acted like a strutting cock as Bajig was doing when he was in charge of the camp. His uncle told Bajig he was to take charge of the camp and he did in his own way.

Two geologists, Tegshe and Gerle are also in the camp and they will take over from Sumiya who is to leave with us and return to UB so he can celebrate the first cutting of his daughter's hair.

Bajig, the rooster, strutted around his hen house pecking at small things left and right, exerting his power demonstrably so everyone knew who was the boss.

"Get me a cup so I can drink tea," he ordered.

He would sit in front of the TV so he could watch the wrestling while the others had to sit so they could see around him. The true colours of a leader surface in a crisis. Most people fail to reach their full potential or show their resilience under stress. They abrogate their responsibilities by fading into the background despite their previous cockiness and extroversion. And so it was with the rooster when our camp faced a crisis.

When the water truck was eventually towed back into camp at 5am in the morning and was sitting idle in the driller's camp the rooster, Bajig was nowhere to be seen. He knew supplying water to the rig was the most important problem needing a solution. The engine in the water truck had not been replaced as I was led to believe it would be by the time it came back to camp. A decision had been made (by somebody!) to use the engine in the towing truck to replace the one in the water tanker.

Drilling had stopped about midnight when the water supply had run out. No more coring would be possible until more water was carted to the drilling site. Therefore, getting the water truck's engine replaced was a high priority. My idea was to fill the water tanker and tow it to the rig, unload the water so they could drill another day while the engines of the trucks were changed. No! The drillers did not want to do it.

Instead, no water was transported and the rig sat idle. By 10am a crew of nine men including Ganana, the assistant cook, were dismantling two truck engines. This activity all took place in a random fashion with no leadership, just men picking a task they could do and then doing it. The excavator driver walked to his machine and brought it back to camp so it could lift the engines.

Out of frustration I took a long walk. Why did it take four days to tow the water truck back to camp? It turns out it was the drilling supervisor and not the rooster, Bajig who had become so annoyed by the delays he had ordered someone to get the water truck. I saw Bajig watching the wrestling when I came back from my walk. He was enjoying the games and not interested in the the mechanical tasks.

I planned showing the proposed drill hole locations to Tegshe and Gerle and explaining the rationale for the drilling program before we left camp on Wednesday morning to drive to Bayankhongor via Gobi-Altai. From there the intention was to drive to UB. The trip would take two days.

Tuesday 13 July.

Mongolia is a country for men. They spit, smoke, slurp, snore, defecate and urinate and don't worry about anything. Sheep, goats and cattle rank beneath men because they can be slaughtered and eaten, or milked and sheared. Dogs and women rank on the lowest rung of society because they can be abused. Women are raped, beaten and serve as slaves to men and animals. Bashed wives who flee to shelters may be killed when they eventually return home.

Social programs are being introduced to change these traditional attitudes, but the battle for transformation has only just begun. Dogs roam free and are malnourished, eating kitchen scraps and whatever they can scrounge.

Exceptions do exist and Kulan and Ganana, the couple who live and work at the camp share work and responsibilities and appear to live as a harmonious couple. Kulan is the cook and Ganana applies his multi-talented skills to handyman tasks as well as mechanical and dish washing chores.

With the water truck functioning and the storage tanks overflowing with water the hydraulic head of the drilling unit decided it would cease moving. Progress on the drill hole stopped yet again. This time it took ten hours to get the rig operating again.

The long drive to Bayankhongor took about 16 hours. In UB I hoped I could settle into a routine of work, writing and relaxation. It certainly was an experience living for twelve days in a ger in remote Mongolia. I learned a lot, but on reaching UB it was time to do what I came to do; review reports and select new projects for investment.

My Unfortunate Friend

My unfortunate friend, a colleague of Tom's has been married more times than he cares to remember. All his divorces cost him a fortune. He has also had many one-night stands and cannot seem to find the 'right' woman to settle down with. Not that he is unattractive. He is intelligent and handsome, but flawed. His past relationships have been dictated by using his eyes and the appendage between his legs to make decisions about the woman of his dreams. He disputes this by saying he does give serious thought to the woman with whom he wants a relationship. I remind him to reflect on his past expeditions into the realm of female relationships he has had, so he could draw some valuable lessons.

For instance, he told me he broke up with a buxom brunette who taught schoolchildren in Darwin after spending several weeks engaged in hot sex, drunken parties and excursions to tourist attractions. Helen was a friend of Jocelyn's. I knew them both and also why Helen discontinued her relationship with Tom. She had found someone else offering greater prospects and felt reluctant to tell Tom she wanted a new relationship.

Then there was the big breasted blonde; another school teacher who smoked and liked horse riding. He never knew why she did not return his phone calls after they had been dating for six weeks. This was Simone, a friend of Ailsa's. Maybe it was simply because he said he was leaving town to do field work in a remote place in northern Australia and she did not want to wait around for him.

A red head with large bosoms, flashy smile and strong personality encouraged him to make a house visit. She then educated him about performing various sex acts to her satisfaction, and his. Her strong personality and powerful attraction seduced him into believing he was truly in love with this wonderful woman. Months passed and the smile on his face never faded because of the frequency of sex and the attention the red-head focused on his anatomy. She also liked the money he earned and the ease with which he handed it over so she could buy all sorts of things she really didn't need, but which she felt made her feel better.

That relationship busted up when it finally dawned on Tom she was just exploiting him. All she wanted was continual sexual gratification and he obliged regularly. She demanded he be available all the time to perform, but when he needed to travel for work they argued. She pestered him to return home so she could enjoy extended periods of sex to fulfil her pent up desire. She needed his body or some other man's and without daily doses of sex she could not exist. Fleeing overseas my unfortunate friend, Tom escaped the torture of living with a nymphomaniac.

Outside Gate Six

My driver stopped outside gate 6 at terminal 3, Peking International airport. He unloaded the heavier of two bags and I took the lighter one. He found a luggage trolley nearby and placed the bag on it. I put the smaller one on top. We shook hands and I thanked him in my badly pronounced Mandarin.

"Xie Xie," I said.

He smiled, closed the trunk, got back in the car and drove off. I pushed the luggage trolley through the automatically opening doors and down the ramp to the departure concourse. Few people were about. A group of people sat with their luggage near the check in desk of Mongolian Airlines, the carrier to fly my bags and me to Ulaanbaatar to start my contract as Exploration Manager.

I found a seat and organised my luggage and carry-on bags. I had four hours to wait before the check in counter opened for my scheduled 1.10am flight. After reading for about thirty minutes, I was disturbed by the arrival of a large group of red capped Chinese tourists and their luggage trolleys loaded with baggage. They shoved their trolleys in chaotic excitement in a disorganised rabble near the check in counters for Emirates Airlines. This throng of surging passengers unsettled the group I was sitting with and we broke up. I decided to stroll with my baggage and headed for the information screen displaying international flights departing the terminal.

On reaching the display screen, I noticed the information changed regularly from English to Mandarin making reading of the information a challenge. I watched as the screen informed me of a flight to Frankfurt at 1.20am, but I could not see my flight listed. Concerned by this and as my previous flight had already been cancelled because of a strike by Mongolian Airlines engineers the previous day, I went to the information desk. They could not confirm the schedule of a Mongolian flight. The attractive Chinese attendant gave me a telephone number of the Mongolian Airlines office in Beijing to call. I dialled the number but received an error message from China Unicom, the mobile phone carrier. I checked with the attendant whether the number was correct. It was. She looked for another number and found one for the office in Mongolia. I tried it with the same unsuccessful result.

The information attendant then suggested I follow her to the main information desk where they have a range of technological devises allowing them better access to information. I duly followed her across the concourse. Another large group of travellers moved snake like across the terminal floor to another check in desk. We avoided them as we walked to the Information Desk.

There, another attendant tried the telephone numbers on a printed folder of papers. All her attempts were unsuccessful. Several people interrupted her searches to ask questions of other flights. Eventually she said I needed to go to the floor below to the Mongolian Airlines office. I was about to leave when her phone rang and she said, "Wait, please sir."

I waited. She took the call and then hung up her phone. She explained I should go to Gate 6 because a Mongolian Airlines agent was waiting for me. I thanked her and wheeled my trolley and bags to the gate. On exiting the building at Gate 6 two men approached to confirm my identity. They said the 1.10am flight to Ulaanbaatar (UB) was cancelled and instead they would take me to a hotel. I was required to follow them. With three other people and their baggage I walked back down the ramp. As we reached the concourse we met a woman who was talking on the cell phone who, when she saw me, asked for my name. I gave it. She repeated it. Then repeated it on the phone to whomever she was talking with. She looked at me, smiled, then said, "I have been looking for you. Follow me."

Another woman, an agent with Mongolian Airlines joined us and we walked down another ramp, took an elevator to a lower level and emerged onto one of the levels of an immense and busy underground car park. We walked out to the edge of a lane way and one of the men indicated we should stop. We did. A few minutes later, a dark Pajero arrived and the three other people who had also joined us packed their luggage into the trunk. The three passengers and one of the men who had met me outside of terminal 3 got in the car. I was left with the two female agents. They were waving their arms and talking, trying to remember where they had parked their car. Their cell phones rang. They answered, gesticulating wildly in the air as they explained what was happening. Then, one woman left followed shortly by the second one who wandered off after indicating for me to stay.

I waited. I saw one of the women talking with a car park attendant. She waved her arms about. He pointed in a direction opposite to where she had waved her arm. She then walked along a lane way where cars were exiting the parking lot. After a few minutes the first woman waved to me from the side of a white Toyota land cruiser, indicating she wanted me to join them. The white car had reversed back up the lane way and had stopped just in front of the Pajero. I wheeled my trolley there and the woman helped me load my bags onto the back seat. After reorganising the bags so she could sit in one of the two seats I sat in the front while she got in the back.

We then drove slowly out of the lot. The driver's cell rang and she answered. Our car almost hit another one reversing into a parking space. The agent drove slowly and erratically to the end of the exit lane way and then steered into the narrow lane connecting the parking lot to the main driveway exit. We edged slowly down the ramp as the driver talked on the cell phone. She drove to the exit pay gates, but stopped two car lengths behind another car at the toll gate. After the driver had paid and drove his car forwards we remained stationary. Our driver was focused on answering the phone. Talking rapidly in Mongolian she attempted to find the electronic toll device in the side pocket of the car as she steered the car towards the barrier, also while rolling down her window. She stopped just before colliding with the barrier gate. She waved the toll device at a metal plate alongside the toll collector's window. A red light turned green, signalling the toll was paid and we could go. When the gate arm lifted she drove out of the lot and onto the exit ramp. Once we had cleared the main traffic area and after conferring with her colleague in the back seat the agent stopped the car and they exchanged places. It turned out the original driver was not competent driving the vehicle.

By then, the car behind us with the man and three passengers had moved ahead of us, so we followed them. We almost lost sight of them as we joined the merging line of vehicles on the highway outside the airport. Farther down the highway, a red light prevented us from following the other car. When the light turned green, we sped up and caught sight of the other car parked on the side of the highway with its emergency flashing lights on. We stopped behind it. Then we waited. Both women made and answered many calls during thirty minutes we were parked on the edge of the busy road. Fast moving traffic flowed past us on the highway. Planes took off from an adjacent runway and the sound of their engines made communication difficult. Eventually a small dark sedan pulled alongside the car in front. The driver turned on the emergency flashing lights then stepped from the car to walk over to the driver of the car I was in. They conversed in Mongolian. The flashing lights on his car stopped functioning. Only the rear red lights indicated to drivers of cars whizzing past us his car was there. Truck drivers blasted their horns. It was a wonder the three cars did not initiate an accident. After a few minutes we followed the small sedan.

I understood the hotel was near the airport, but we drove on a long highway for many minutes before turning, then turning again and driving for long distances again. We took a short dirt back road to link to another highway. Meanwhile, both women answered and made many calls on their cellular phones. Some in broken Mandarin were apparently misunderstood by the person on the other end of the call because the women repeated themselves many times in order to be understood. Other calls were in rapid fire Mongolian, their native tongues. Between calls, they talked frantically between themselves. Obviously, the management of the stranded passengers was not going smoothly. I joked I thought they were driving us to UB. They did not think it funny.

The journey clearly demonstrated to me it is not recommended to drive while talking on a cell phone. Apart from several near collisions the driver managed to weave all across several lanes to the annoyance of passing cars and trucks. We almost ran up the back of the car in the centre of the convoy. The lead sedan had its lights on flashing, so was easy to follow. We also had our emergency lights flashing. The convoy moved as one, crossing intersections on red lights, turning across on-coming traffic which slowed to let us turn, and steadily moving at slow speed down highways. It was exciting, exhilarating and potentially dangerous. I wondered where in the hell we were going.

At 9.45 pm, and after having been on the road for an hour since we had met the driver of the small sedan we eventually arrived down a long dusty lane at a hotel. The Beijing Dragon Club lays a long way from the airport even though it seemed we had driven around almost in a circle. It looked almost like a disused hotel just re-opened to cater for us, and it is nowhere near any shops and cafes, but in the rural surrounds of Beijing. The use of the word, cater, is too strong for it implies a degree of service, but by the time I arrived the other stranded passengers who had been transferred from the first hotel earlier in the day had consumed all the food, most of the water and were steadily imbibing the remaining beer. People were milling around the entrance and I could see they had been drinking beer and other refreshments for some time because of the empty bottles strewn around on the driveway. I recognised several faces from the crowd on the bus the first night when the flight was cancelled.

One of the men who had met me at the airport explained in Mongolian the 1am flight had been cancelled and the company was offering a refund of the air ticket. It is what I found out following translation from one of the passengers. The representative also suggested they could fly people to the Chinese border and then they could take the train to Ulaanbaatar from there. Many people had questions. Some people wanted to accept the offer. After about an hour when the questioning had ended, I asked about my revised travel plan.

"A moment," he said, walking away into the dark recesses of the garden in front of the hotel. So, I asked one of the female agents who had driven me in the car. Same reply.

I mingled with other passengers and we joked about what was happening to us. We talked about UB and the social circumstances, economy and politics. People who would not normally talk to each other suddenly became friends. We talked about our families, the work we did and why we were going to UB and where we had been. All of these conversations passed the time while we waited to learn some degree of meaning and direction out of the activities of the airline agents. None seemed forthcoming and before going to bed at 12.15am I asked for a telephone number of their office so I could call to find out about flights for the next day. I was given the number with the uncertain advice about flights operating in the next few days.

It turned out the Mongolian Government had sacked the Board of the company because they had fired all striking engineers and then installed a new Board. They employed some Korean engineers so they could get planes flying again because without an engineer saying a plane is safe to fly the planes could not take off. There was talk about putting everyone on an Air China flight the next day, but later the plan failed to materialise because no seats were available. It was then suggested we could fly to Seoul and transfer to a Korean Air flight going to UB. They would look into it. It was further suggested a Korean Air plane could fly to Beijing, pick us up and continue to Mongolia. The plan was eliminated quickly because of the politics between China and Korea, and the Chinese not wanting Korean planes flying passengers in China.

My booking was changed so I would fly out of Beijing to Vancouver. Having overstayed my one-day entry visa into China I was required to explain to a half a dozen immigration officers why I had stayed too long in Beijing. It would be another three months before I returned and continued my journey to Ulaanbaatar. I did not visit Gate 6, but made the connecting flight without complication.

Retrogressive Metamorphism

Parents, family and friends metamorphose instantly in front of a new born baby. Like magic or spellbound, humans change from sedate, often unsmiling rational (for most of us!) individuals into excited, incoherent blabberers who gush beaming smiles and prod and poke the infant while uttering nonsensical phrases and sounds. "Goo goo, gaa gaa," flow freely from our mouths while we wave our heads like an Indian (from India) conversing to a friend. Have you ever been to India? If you have then you know what I'm talking about. If not, then this might provoke you to arrange travel there to experience the cultural mannerisms for yourself. But I digress.

The new born can become frightened by the large bug-eyed human shape moving strangely before their unfocused eyes. In and out and back and forth the two large eyes may move. A prominent snout juts forward into their little faces intimidating them to shock. Such fight may lead to screaming cries. Wide white bars of lines shift up and down and in and out, making anyone prone to motion sickness throw up, let alone a baby who has never seen teeth, tongue and lips at close range. No wonder the infant bursts into tears and screams; a scary monster is about to eat their face!

"Get the thing away from my face!" they would shout if they knew the words and could speak. Their brains probably scream the sentiment and try to make the sounds of words they have heard in muffled tones through amniotic fluids during the preceding months. While slowly growing in the womb the child has heard varieties of sounds; conversations and music and made connections to form in a rapidly evolving brain. Once born their brain has to deal with the harsh reality of loud incoherent sounds, sharply pitched unintelligible words. Often these are associated with bright light and quizzical forms suddenly looming within millimetres of their face, before disappearing just as quickly. It is all too strange to comprehend. Uncontrollable natural bodily functions loosen bowels and urinate, as well as scream.

Intestinal tracts and bladders do not think, but operate automatically when natural triggers release commands to open flood gates and valves, allowing the flow of fluids and slurries. The infant's brain has not been trained to control those engineering commands, so independent actions occur. Gaseous eruptions accompany the partitioning of solid and liquid matter. A sphincter opens and relieves the back pressure of the solid obstructions. The consistency of the output depends on the nature of the input, but a kaleidoscope of colour, texture, and odour emerges.

Adults need to assist the child otherwise the kicking legs become covered in excrement and urine, leading to sores, sickness and likely death. Diapers or nappies need regular changing and parents do this reluctantly, but with due diligence and care, knowing the screams from an uncomfortable baby will cease once the infant is clean and dry, and well nourished. It is a cycle; food and milk in the mouth and faeces and urine from the other end. It is nature's way of ensuring the child lives. As my crude brother used to say to his great joy, "If you don't eat, you don't shit, and if you don't shit you die!"

Some brothers know everything, but I wish they would not express all their thoughts out loud! Humans retrograde with age. This is indisputable. It is something we cannot change despite all the advances in medical science. Eventually, if we live long enough and have not done anything stupid to remove us from the Darwinian line of continual reproduction we lose the capacity to look after ourselves and require assistance as if we have become an infant again. As dementia or physical incapacity control our lives we need carers to perform the menial tasks of our daily ablutions. We become infants; incontinent and frightened. It's not the scariness of the eyes, teeth and smiles bearing in on us but the lack of recognition of their ownership. Without a carer we are helpless. We metamorphose into an unhealthy mass of useless flesh. We need to give thanks to nurses and carers because they ensure we live in a dignified manner at the end of our lives, and receive as much attention at the end as the start of life.

Nurses and carers are often unappreciated and deserve recognition for the roles they play in the critical periods of our lives when we are vulnerable and defenceless. As humans the retrogressive metamorphism we experience late in life is probably more painful and depressing than at any other period because we know what it was like to independently manage our bodies, thoughts and words. As we approach our life's terminus our tongues flap uselessly in our mouths as the link between brain and muscle dissipates into inarticulate mumbles. The sphincters and valves we once controlled no longer respond automatically, but work when natural forces exceed a resistant threshold.

My friend Anne is a carer. She cared for her father during the last few years of his life. She also cared for her mother. Anne trained to become a doctor and except for an illness late in her final year, which robbed her of a medical degree, she would have graduated as a doctor and served many patients well. Initially, she worked as a nurse and then studied long and hard at an unachievable goal. The years spent caring for both parents, one after the other, eroded her bank savings, deprived her of careers and strained her own health.

Anne is my hero. There must be many like her, but we do not hear about them or their stories. The news is always bad and of criminals, disasters, politics and the economy. Society is a mess when priorities exclude people in need. Greed, gluttony and the desire for power and influence seem to control people's lives when taking care of infants and the elderly should be uppermost.

"Wait until you get old," my mother used to say, "then you will realise first-hand what it is like to experience retrogressive metamorphism."

* * *

Retrograde metamorphism is a change in the mineral assemblage and the composition of a rock, occurring during release of pressure and cooling to reconstitute a relatively high-grade metamorphic rock.

The morning orchestra

At a rural property near Santa Fe, New Mexico.

A thin white frost coats the ground and finches, scrub jays, juncos and magpies swoop onto platforms and bars to eat seeds in self-feeders. Long triangular transparent ice crystals inter-grown with small slender translucent needles form a thin fragile shield over the stock tanks. A sharp cool southerly breeze chills the air and whistles through the piñon pines.

A tall grey balding man looks out from a large kitchen window and admires the early rays of the yellow sunrise as they illuminate the morning scene at the bird feeders. His mistress is upstairs. She is his beautiful princess. This morning she is catching a few extra minutes sleep. Lying snug beneath warm woollen blankets pulled up under her chin she sleeps in their stucco home. Warm air wafts upwards to the mezzanine floor bedroom from a fire he has just lit in the lounge.

Her tousled blonde hair spills loosely across a crumpled white pillow. Small soft hands and strong fingers, two bearing silver rings, loosely grip the sheets around her tender white neck. Her hands, now soft, conceal many strenuous hours of manual labour. Her rosy cheeks on her pale angelic face angle peacefully upwards towards the yellow stained timber ceiling. Her radiant green eyes hide behind creaseless eyelids edged by long pale lashes. An unobservant onlooker might think her gaze is on the knotted wood ceiling above her head, but her shuttered eyes enable views of other vistas within her mind. Dreams appear vividly in her deep sleep and then noisily disappear, like the sounds vibrating rhythmically from her open mouth.

He leaves the window and sits at the table in the dining room below the bedroom. It seems to him from the slow repetitive sounds she makes an invisible carpenter is meticulously sawing wood for a cabinet or desk. Her melodious tones cease momentarily before renewing with strength and energy. As he approaches he hears a saw make another series of cuts. He thinks it sounds like a crosscut saw. Its teeth tearing through the wooden fibres in each stroke, reducing a long plank to size. The sound changes volume with every cut as if the carpenter has deliberately altered the stroke to match the texture of the wood. Each pause between the cuts enables the carpenter to measure the stroke before pushing the blade once more through the timber.

He listens intently and amusingly while he silently spoons oatmeal into his hungry mouth. He has made a large bowl of his favourite breakfast and brewed a pot of strong Ethiopian coffee. He likes the combination of nutritious cereal washed down with a fortifying drink to energise him for his work. The cooking recipe he follows is simple; a handful of sun-dried Flame raisins mixed with a watery slurry of traditional oatmeal seasoned with a pinch of ocean salt. Cooked slowly on low heat while stirring rhythmically in the shape of the infinity sign relaxes and hypnotises. At the point of boiling of the mixture, he turns off the stove and removes the pan to rest awhile. Garnished with sliced bananas and a spoonful of brown sugar, he completes the food. The hot oatmeal melts the sugar causing brown streaks to spread as he turns the mixture over in his bowl.

He looks at the dogs lying silently on the floor and couch, listening to the snoring sounds their mistress makes above. Her rhythmical low tonal sounds, like softly sawing wood, calm their ears and induce a drowsy state. They lazily rest in the warm air surrounding the fire burning cedar. Their behaviour this morning replaces the usual boisterous activity, toy evisceration, and barking as they listen and join in the musical ensemble.

Wally, a one-eyed Australian Blue Heeler-Labrador cross, spreads her body sideways on a rug under a long, engraved lounge table. She joins in the carpentry orchestra with her mistress by emitting periodic sounds like a tenon saw sharply cutting joints. The resonating chorus has a different tone and pitch to her mistress, and is shorter. Old Wally produces a different tone of lower volume, but blends in to harmonise with the sounds from the bedroom above. Her contribution is as though another carpenter is using a fine fret saw to shape a piece of sawn timber. She changes the tool. Now it sounds to him like Wally has selected a small plane to shape the rough surface in short repetitive strokes, shaving millimetres from the wood.

At the dining room table, he takes another mouthful of oatmeal and chews on a succulent Flame raisin. It has absorbed fluid and expanded into a plump delicious grape. The intense taste and fleshy texture adds zest to his meal. He pauses to enjoy the fruity sensations and listen to the carpenters at work. The sounds have changed as if different saws are cutting along the grain: a rip saw shaping smaller pieces and a tenon saw accurately cutting joints. A plane is smoothing and straightening edges.

Gus, a poodle has tucked himself hard against one of two pillows on the red velvet couch. His mistress thought Gus looked like her male companion: longish curly white hair and big ears. Gus's ears are long and floppy. In contrast, her companion's ears, though prominent, do not hang loosely, but angle sharply upwards through tufts of grey curly hair from his tanned and stubbled face. Gus's voice this morning is subtle unlike his personality. Resting silently, he becomes a different animal. His exuberant personality is subdued. The rhythm of his breathing merges softly with the other sounds. The timing of his sighs coincides with the sawing notes. It usually comes just as the duo cease their tunes.

Thackeray, a big black Labrador, lies sprawled alongside the slow combustion wood stove. His chest rises and falls in time with the saw cuts he hears. The air rushes in and out through moist nostrils and produces alternating long and short rasping notes, like a fine jeweller's file delicately working silver. Longer or shorter and deeper breaths change the tune and break the rhythm. The harmony is lost in a pulse, but it does not matter because the orchestra plays on. Soon they are all back in breathtaking synchronicity.

As the grey haired man gradually eats his way towards the bottom of the bowl of oatmeal, he listens to the regularity of the breathing about him and to the orchestral ensemble's rhythmical tones. He savours the best coffee he has made. They had decided to reduce the quantity of water in the coffee percolator so as not to waste the remaining cup, which always seemed there after breakfast. His task today was to judge the reduction in coffee grounds he measured into the paper filter to match the reduced volume of water. Today he has judged it perfectly. All he has to do tomorrow and every day afterwards is remember the number of spoons of fresh grounds he has used: nine.

His princess dreams on, oblivious to the orchestra she leads. Her rhythmical breathing and carpenter's tune she makes conforms to the sounds of the ocean as she imagines herself standing transfixed by the regularity of waves crashing onto a coarse sandy beach. She dreams she is watching a yacht bobbing on the swell out at sea. She wishes she were sailing across the Atlantic Ocean to Ireland. Her thoughts and breaths ebb and flow as though her body were in unison with the rise and fall of each swell.

She sees herself sailing the yacht across the sea and riding each swell. She tacks into the wind until it dies to a breeze, then stops. Her breathing pauses before restarting as once again the carpenter begins cutting delicate joints in series with a dovetail saw. The pitch seems higher and the volume less intense. Each cut shorter than before. Then after a break, a different saw begins to cut again, shaping more wood for new furniture.

In her dreams, the pulsating movement of the sea gives way to sensuous stroking. She now adores how her lover's fingers caress her body in rhythmical waves. His breath in tune with hers, or it's what she imagines. From her belly, his hand moves upwards along her ribs to her breast. Not tickling, but sensuously engaging. There it pauses to caress and fondle before moving across her chest to the other breast where again in time with her breathing his fingers gently massage a nipple. His hand moves sensuously down her ribs and across her belly in waves of pure pleasure until they reach her leg. There his hand pauses briefly before sliding smoothly across her inner thigh and upwards to her velvet vee. His sensitive hand on her pubic hair sends ripples of ecstasy tingling up her spine.

Fabulous feelings sweep in waves along her back and to her brain. *Keep going. Keep the rhythm. Move your hands and stimulate me more,* she dreams. On it goes the never ending rippling of pleasure. He keeps the cycle going and her stimulation increases. Then, as the pleasure mounts throughout her body and reaches a climax, her breathing changes pitch. A new saw cuts through her senses and in another pulse, she is in a different scene.

Her new emotion becomes more animated. She is riding her mare at a canter through a pine forest along a trail winding between the scented trees and through the mossy rocks. Her blonde hair trails in the wind as she bounces in rhythm with each stride. Gusts of air brush her skin as the rotating fan by her bed blasts intermittent streams of refreshing wind. Between the trees, she feels the sun upon her face. Her smile grows wider and beams with joy as together they leap a fallen tree and race down a slope to a dry creek crossing. They slow to catch the beat of the saw cuts and change pace to pull hard and exhale deeply to ascend an imaginary hill. The sawing sounds slow, then stop.

Below he listens to the notes. Would the music start again? Wally and Gus maintain the beat and then the carpenter takes up the saw again and on they slowly go climbing the hill. She stops to admire the view across the forest to the mesa, which she loves, and the sawing slows. It does not stop, but draws longer cuts with lengthy pauses in between as she admires the spectacle of steep forested slopes above red-layered strata. The rugged mesa cliff against the cloudless deep blue sky forms a painter's dream of colour contrast and perspective.

Wally shakes her head. One ear twitches. Is she dreaming too? Perhaps she's reacting to a rabbit on the run, a raven in the field, or something else she is dreaming in her mind. She flinches and changes her breathing. A new rhythm begins with different tone and speed as if she were trotting along a path or chasing small game through the trees. Maybe she imagines she is in a forest surrounded by tall Ponderosa pines and sees or hears a sound nearby which startles her awake. Suddenly she raises her head and stands shakily on all fours. Disturbed by something in her dream she shifts place once more. Regaining a comfortable spot, she closes her eyes and joins the orchestra again. Her breathing steady, her mind relaxed she plays a slightly different tune than before.

The sawing carpenter stops at the end of a short sharp cut and brings the music to a halt. The catalyst to end the symphony is indiscernible. He had finished eating and was listening, but he could not sense why the music stopped. He never heard a bark, a noise, a rustle at the door, or a raven calling from the piñon top. He only heard a raven sliding down the metal roof in an attempt to gain balance; it's scratching claws producing a screeching climax like metal scraping symbols. This high-pitched sound stirs Gus into action. The poodle shakes his head vigorously from side to side as he wakes. Then repeatedly, barking loudly, he takes responsibility for the reveille, bugling the awakening call.

The morning orchestra stops playing. The carpenters lay down their tools. Listening as he arises from the table the grey haired man hears the bed covers fold and then the sound of a few light footsteps on the floor above his head. He knows the performance has ended without applause. His princess, wearing a dark blue cashmere nightgown, steps lightly onto the rug at the bottom of the spiral wooden stairs.

"Good morning!" she says with a beaming smile which spreads across her face. She slowly takes in the scene with bleary eyes. They all stir in response. Their mistress they adore and love is finally awake. It is all that matters. It is all they sense. A snoring session, deep slumber, carpenters at work or an orchestral performance no longer matters. What does, is the woman they love is awake and amongst them again. She spreads her enduring love and affection equally on them all. With the concert now over a new day has begun.

The Trans-Siberian Experience

It was January, 1978 when I travelled east to west across the USSR on the Trans-Siberian train. I had taken a flight from Sydney to Tokyo and stayed for two nights in a hotel in downtown Tokyo. After a disorientating walk in the streets I needed to take a train two stations to return to my hotel precinct. Not knowing the language and unable to read the signs made it a challenging exercise, but fortunately someone I met spoke English and gave me good directions.

The next day a bus took a group of us, five men; three Aussies, one Spaniard and one German, and four Australian women to a ship berthed at a Yokohama dock. I remember the traffic, smoke spewing from industrial stacks and unreadable signs. Our bags were taken from the bus and loaded on board the *Star of Lenin.* Passports and visas were checked by the Purser and then we were shown our cabins. I shared a room, tiny with a small window, allowing a restricted view outside. The regular beat of diesel engines throbbed through the structure.

I explored the ship and soon found the pair of Aussies at the bar drinking beer. I joined them for the first of many alcoholic gatherings. Once underway we strolled briefly on the deck, but did not stay long in the freezing wind, sweeping across the upper deck. Russian sailors and female cleaners sat in sheltered nooks to smoke and talk.

Soon the Aussie women felt the motion of the vessel and succumbed to sea-sickness. The men ate dinner and drank more beer oblivious to the movements of the ship. Our first taste of Russian food did not impress; oily borscht, a watery mix of several olives, slices of beetroot and a fatty oily scum came served in a metal bowl accompanied by hard brown bread we soon nicknamed 'cardboard.' The main meal was a small greasy meat patty with a dollop of mashed potato, one partly fried egg, a slice of pale yellow cheese and a large green pickle. Dessert consisted of a dark chocolate slice so hard a nail could not be hammered through without great difficulty. I'm not kidding!

Thankfully we only ate one dinner on board, but breakfast and lunch the next day were not much better. The bar saw more customers.

My male companions were two mechanics from South Australia. They had spent weeks in the Philippines and Thailand enjoying the red light districts and learning about Asian women; you understand! I heard of their exploits and of their drunken orgies, and related my quiet tales of work and cricket. Boring!! Alcohol bound us together in a jovial, care-free trio. We would later prove a handful for our Russian Intourist guide.

On arrival at Nakhodka the harbour was clogged with large chunks of floating ice. We berthed at a frozen wharf covered in white snow and ice. Then, unlike now, Vladivostok was off-limits to foreigners because of the cold-war between the West and Communism. We passed through Customs and Immigration. Our passports were stamped. I temporarily misplaced my passport and almost panicked worrying about interrogation and possible confinement in Siberia. I had forgotten I had put the passport in a folder where normally I only kept money, and was relieved to find it after anxious searches through my luggage.

Once through the Immigration barrier we met our guide who would take us across the USSR, from east to west. Her name was Natasha Yevtushenko, a dark haired woman in her late twenties, like us, with an attractive round face, dark eyes and unsmiling mouth. She spoke good English with a cute accent, and I fell in 'love' immediately. This trip was going to be fun!

We took a bus to the train station after porters had loaded our luggage. It was sub-zero and snowing lightly as we walked across the platform to a carriage before being shown to our compartments. The four women shared one cubicle, the two Aussie mechanics had a booth with two beds, and I shared another compartment with the Spaniard, German and Natasha.

The four berth cubicles had two long bench seats. At night these formed the lower beds. Two more beds were fastened to the wall above the bench seats and these were rotated lower for sleeping. The two berth cubicle had two bench seats converted into beds. The matron of the carriage, who spoke no English issued sheets and blankets, and indicated tea would be brewed all day on her samovar. We could help ourselves and we did. Glasses for tea were stored in a small unit near her kitchen.

Alongside the kitchen was a small cubicle with a hole in the floor below a seat. It served as the ablution. A small basin and sink allowed for the maintenance of a basic element of hygiene, although the tap leaked only drizzles of water. This would be our home for the next few weeks while on board the train. We needed to adjust to the lack of space, the smell, noises and rocking of the carriage.

Thankfully, we stopped at towns along the way to visit scenes, historic buildings, memorials to the dead and small museums. At those times we shared hotel rooms with long wide beds, high ceilings and enormously long bath robes. The towels reached the floor while being held with arms outstretched above the head. Food in the hotels was generally much better than on the train; not wonderful, just better, more edible.

It was evening when the train pulled out of Nakhodka and we made our beds and tried to fall asleep in harmony with the lurching of the train. I must have slept quite well because light poured through the window as Natasha tugged my arm to inform me breakfast was ready in the dining car.

Breakfast matched the service on the ferry. An entree of cheese, salami and olives was followed by a partly cooked egg, slice of ham and hard thin bread. Tea saved the meal and by adding sugar it gave me a lift. We could not believe the small size or poor quality of the meal and joked about it until we laughed to ease the discomfort.

The train sped along and we adjourned to the Aussie mechanics room, which had more space than the four-berth compartment. Out came the cards, glasses and a bottle of scotch. We proceeded to play

Five Hundred and drink. The wintry landscape passed us by and little changed when we looked out and saw what we had seen before. In another compartment the Aussie women played scrabble and talked about who they were and where they were from. Natasha kept a close eye on us, probably to form an opinion about each one of us and to see we did not misbehave.

At Khabarovsk we disembarked and travelled by bus to a hotel situated on the edge of a square. The room was heated, with large, high ceilings and three layers of glass in the windows. Outside was bitterly cold, and in the morning during a walk in the low angle of the sun an elderly woman came up to me and, pointing at her head said, " холодно" (Kholodno = cold). Repeating this several times and then pointing to me, I interpreted her gesticulations to mean my head would get cold and I needed to cover it up. While I had bought a sheepskin jacket to keep my body warm I had not thought about a hat or scarf. So, when I saw the four Aussie women I asked if they had a spare beanie I could borrow until I could go to a store and buy a hat. One of them produced a knitted brown beanie; cute!! Just the fashion thing for a rugged Aussie male!!

The children I saw as I walked in the square were playing in the snow and building snowmen. They were bundled up with several layers and looked like small round lumpy balls with a pair of eyes sticking out. They all wore mitts and thick insulated boots, things I did not have either!!

As a group we met a local guide who showed us historic homes, museums and a memorial to the people killed during the Second

World War and in the earlier war against Japan. This was the first of many eternal flames we saw across the country. We were constantly reminded of the suffering endured by the Russian people during various wars and of their heroic victories. Tens of millions of Russians died during WWII, and their descendants would not forget them. We would not either.

After dinner we attended a disco bar in the hotel where a band played and we could dance. We watched for a while and as they were playing western music we danced with the locals. Several couples wanted to talk to us on the dance floor, but when the music stopped they returned to their seats. We went to our table. This happened several times until we swapped partners and I danced with the wife of one of the Russian men. We then joined them at their table and shared a drink.

A group of Russian soldiers at another table saw us drinking vodka and sent a bottle to us via the waiter. When it arrived the waiter indicated the source of the gift and the soldiers smiled and waved and indicated for us to drink it. We took the cap off and saluted them several times with shots of the potent clear liquid.

As the night wore on, the couple we had joined wanted to talk to us some more. They indicated we should follow them to their apartment nearby where we could talk without the loud background music. I went with one of the Aussie women and the two Aussie mechanics. The rest of the group went to their rooms and bed.

A sentry sat at the top of the stairs of each floor of the Russian couple's apartment and they observed our presence. The couple showed us into their small three room apartment and offered us drinks and tea. Before the samovar had boiled the telephone rang and the host answered. He frowned and put the phone down. A few minutes later just as we were heavily engaged in conversation the phone rang again. The host spent several minutes on the phone, and then, after hanging up, informed us we had to leave or they would be in trouble with the authorities. The security agents had reported the couple fraternising with foreigners; an act regarded as subversive, illegal and intolerable. We decided to leave otherwise the couple would be interrogated and punished.

The next day we toured more sites under the ever watchful and mistrustful eye of our Intourist guide who was not happy we had broken protocol by socialising with the locals. How did Natasha know because she was not there?

Later the same night, after a more pleasant dinner at the hotel we boarded a bus and returned to the railway station to catch the next train heading west. The Trans-Siberian is not one train, but a series of trains running each day from east to west. People alight and re-board at cities along the route in an orderly, well managed process under the watchful eye of security, herded along by Intourist guides.

We found our allocated accommodation in a carriage similar to the first one, and shared the cubicles as before. We slept as the train headed to Ulan-Ude.

Next morning after another tasteless breakfast the guys played cards and drank Scotch. Two of our female companions were ill; the food not agreeing with their delicate stomachs. Outside, the white landscape whisked by until we stopped to allow goods trains to travel in the opposite direction. Army tanks and heavy military equipment were being shipped east as tensions with China persisted along the border.

Small villages lined the route. Dark smoke drifted from chimneys of drab wooden houses. People in dark clothes, scarves and hats went about their daily lives. The train stopped to pick up passengers and parcels going west. Shirtless soldiers, braving the cold, ran from the train to buy pine nuts, hot food and confectionery from temporary stalls on the platforms; their breath clouding their faces in the sub-zero temperatures.

It was another night on the train and another day before we reached Ulan-Ude. By then we had settled into a routine of meals, cards and booze. Ulan-Ude is the junction for the rail links through Mongolia to China and the Far East. Another Aussie joined our group, a school teacher from Western Australia who had taken the train from Beijing. For the next few days he related stories about his Chinese adventures. We informed him of our journey so far. He also like playing Five Hundred, so the four of us passed the time together.

Ulan-Ude was a train spotter's Mecca because railway yards contained hundreds of steam locomotives. We were informed the Russians felt it necessary to keep them in case there was a shortage of diesel. They could easily fire them up again because coal was plentiful and readily available.

The Spaniard was an artist. He had married a Japanese woman and had lived in Japan for three years, and was now heading to Seville, his home. He spoke broken English, Spanish and Japanese. He described his art; charcoal drawings of buildings, landscapes and portraits. One of the women asked him to draw a portrait of her, so they spent time together so he could work his magic crayon.

The German had travelled around Australia doing odd jobs and visiting the major tourist attractions. He was heading to Berlin where he intended completing his architectural studies. He spoke German, English, French and a little Russian. At each place we stopped on the trip across the USSR the Spaniard and the German were allocated their own local guide who spoke Spanish or German, respectively. We had our local English-speaking guide. Natasha, our Intourist guide visited the local security office to report on us while we explored the towns with each new local guide.

All the boozing we did had two purposes; men doing what men do, but also medicinal. By the time we reached Ulan-Ude the four women were suffering the ill effects of the food. They rarely ate anything because their stomachs could not handle the food. On the other hand the alcoholic men only slowly succumbed to the poor quality food. I became sick in Moscow, and the last guy to become sick fell ill as we approached Leningrad (St. Petersburg). We attributed our gastric resilience to the alcohol we drank. Nice story, but maybe it was just we had stronger metabolisms!

The train headed to Irkutsk, a city on Lake Baikal, the deepest fresh water lake in the world. Our stop there included a tour of the lake; but it was frozen, so we visited a museum where everything about the lake was explained. Of course, there was another memorial with an eternal flame. More museums related stories about WWII and how the Russians had moved their industries to the east as the Nazis advanced towards Moscow.

At midnight we re-boarded a train and set off for Krasnoyarsk and Novosibirsk. Once on the train one of the Aussie mechanics realised he had left his passport in the hotel room. Oops!! Bugger! He was at the point of panic and required lots of calming down. Eventually he realised there was nothing he could do. Half a bottle of vodka later he fell asleep!

At Krasnoyarsk we followed the usual procedure and took a bus from the station to the hotel. At each hotel we handed in our passports and received the keys to our rooms. Problem! One of us did not have his passport. This would be interesting. We were in for a shock.

Holding up a passport the clerk said, "Mr Aussie tourist is this your passport?"

We almost fainted! How in the hell did his passport turn up in the next hotel before us? Security obviously checked our rooms after we had left, and then sent the document on the train or flew it ahead of us. Wow! We were stunned.

Krasnoyarsk is the third largest city in Siberia. It is an academic and industrial city with a huge aluminium smelter. Political prisoners were exiled there and the town became a centre of the Gulags under Stalin.

On the train from Irkutsk I met a local Russian as I walked to the dining car. He wanted to talk in his broken English to find out about what was happening in the west; about politics and the economy. I started answering his questions, but then a fellow passenger came and tried to drag him away. He resisted and shrugged off the interfering individual. After a few more minutes another passenger came up and tugged at the man's sleeve. Again he resisted, but then a second man stood and pulled at the talkative Russian's arm to drag him away from me. He shouted at them in Russian, but they 'swore' back at him and continued pulling his arms, succeeding in pulling him out of the carriage.

At Novosibirsk we visited Akademgorodok, the educational and scientific city about 20km from the centre of Novosibirsk. It was built in a birch and pine forest, and accommodated politically correct academics who received special food and other benefits while conducting their research. Novosibirsk is Russia's third largest city after Moscow and Leningrad (now called St Petersburg), and formed an integral part of the industrialisation of the Soviet Union.

We visited another memorial, the zoo, historic buildings and saw the changing of the guard at an eternal flame. Monuments to the victims of WWII and a museum celebrating the Red Army victory in the revolution were also featured. Late in the afternoon we walked onto a frozen river to watch ice fishing. We met a tall

Russian man who had chopped a hole in the ice in several places and had fishing lines suspended in the near zero temperature water. My shoes were not meant for standing in the icy conditions and I was happy to return to the warmth of the bus.

Again at midnight we took the train from Novosibirsk to Moscow. Three days later we arrived in Moscow after more adventures on the train with locals trying to make contact with us, but being prevented by other passengers. Clearly, speaking to foreigners was not permitted, but there was nevertheless strong interest in finding out what was happening in the rest of the world.

After breakfast the next morning and a short tour before lunch the Aussie men decided it was time for a beer or two at the hotel bar. We strolled up to the bar and ask the waitress for "четыре пива" (chyetirye peeba), or four beers. The waitress said, "Nyet!"

What? No! We ask again in English and held up four fingers and indicated we wanted a drink by tipping the wrist.

"No!"

What? We are at a bar in a hotel and cannot buy a beer. You must be kidding? No! We found the manager and asked him for four beers. Again no! Why not! The answer was they do not serve single beers at the bar. What? We look at each other and shrug our shoulders. Now what?

I then have a bright idea and ask, "How many beers will you sell us?"

The answer, "A case!" We look at each other, smile and nod, saying, "sure, we'll buy a case."

We pool our cash. The manager went around to the back of the bar and brought out a case of twenty-four cold cans of Heineken. Yippee!!

We took the case to a table around which were four chairs. We tore the top off the case and started drinking the cans. After emptying each can we put the empties in the middle of the table and started to build a pyramid. Passing Scandinavians, who were staying in the hotel, smiled and joked at us as they walked passed. The Aussie women came over and two helped themselves to a beer each. The other two ordered cocktails (no problem with a single cocktail?!). By dinner time only two beer cans were left in the case. That night we went to a concert given by the Red Army Choir and then to a ballet called "Stone Crystal" or some such title.

The following day we visited the GUM, the State Department Store, on Moscow's Red Square. I bought a dark horse hair hat. I still have it today. It replaced the brown knitted beanie I had worn every time we left the train or bus. We lined up to view the body of Lenin lying in state. The line of viewers stretched for several hundred metres. Gradually we filed into the red granite mausoleum and passed the reclining body of Vladimir Ilyich Lenin, who had died in 1924.

That night we visited a Russian Circus, before walking in the freezing streets. I was followed by a chap about my build. Finally, he approached me to ask how much I wanted for my jeans. He wanted to buy them, then and there!! I said no, but he pestered me. Our guide, Natasha saw what was happening and came up to us. She told him to leave, which he did. Then she chastised me for trying to sell stuff to the locals. Bitch!

Later we visited museums, another WWII memorial, watched changing of the guards again at an eternal flame, and drove around the city, having a guide point out various landmarks. That night we got back on the train for Leningrad. Natasha knew precisely what had happened even though she had not accompanied us on the tour.

The hotel in Leningrad was the grandest hotel room I have ever stayed in. Malachite and marble mouldings and fittings decorated the two rooms, which were enormous. In the entry was a very high and ornately decorated ceiling with a crystal chandelier. The bathroom was as big as a normal bedroom, with so much room twenty people could have easily fitted in at the same time. It too contained green malachite and grey-white marble everywhere. A huge mirror about ten feet tall lined one wall. The towels were gigantic, also ten foot long. Was this a room for Russian giants?

Then we visited the most amazing place I have ever been inside; the Winter Palace. It is a massive collection of palaces and adjacent buildings filled with art of every age and description collected since the days of Catherine the Great (1762 - 1796). The palace itself is an architectural and design wonder, but the works of art represent every genre and age of European art possible. It is not possible to see every painting in one day even if you keep walking for eight hours and don't stop to look at a single painting for more than a second. There are rooms after rooms of Renaissance, Impressionist, Modern paintings, and Italian Masters and then there are the sculptures. It's an extravaganza of artistic expression housed in one place. Absolutely magnificent! For me it was the highlight of the journey.

Before we boarded the train to take us out of the USSR I was able to give Natasha a huge kiss to thank her for being such a wonderful guide. At the conclusion of the train journey to Helsinki we crossed the border into Finland. But before we reached the border the train stopped to allow armed Russian guards access to conduct a final inspection. We were asked to step out into the corridor where one guard kept an eye on us while the other guard searched the compartment. Then, one by one we were asked into the compartment and frisked. We had to empty our pockets, but I had forgotten to dispose of a rouble. It turned up when I emptied my pocket. I was questioned about why I had it. What was I doing taking Russian currency out of the country? The coin was confiscated. The guards checked our passports, and then let us back into the compartment.

In contrast, the unarmed Finnish guards, looking more like ticket inspectors, just scanned our passports, smiled and said "welcome." The best part of reaching Finland was the food; fresh milk, juices, bread, and meats and poultry, cheese and freedom. Everyone made gluttons of themselves, and smiled happily, satisfied to have survived the journey.

It would be interesting to re-do the trip after glasnost and perestroika (openness and restructuring) devised by Mikhail Gorbachev, and see how the country is different under a democratic regime of Russia compared to the Communist era of the USSR.

Three sisters

I met Torina in Santa Fe, New Mexico while working as a contract geologist for a uranium exploration company. This is what I remember about one of our conversations.

"There's a postcard for you miss," the concierge said as Torina entered the apartment complex.

"Thanks."

"I'll get it for you."

Torina took off her raincoat, shook it at the doorway to dislodge the Seattle rain and then hung it on the available coat rack. She took off her protective overshoes and placed them carefully next to the coat stand. Then picking up her satchel she walked to the concierge's open door.

As the concierge returned she said, "It's from France, by the look of the stamp."

Torina angrily took the postcard from the nosy concierge and hastily said thanks. Looking at the card she saw a string of tied barges laying at anchor on a river near a bridge. The black and white card also had a church spire in the background. Turning the card over she saw it was from her sister. "Thanks," she said again as she climbed the stairs to her room.

Torina unlocked her door and dropped the satchel on the table nearby. Then, walking slowly across to the kitchen counter top she read the postcard. In a scrawling hand written script she recognised instantly she read:

"Hi, Tori, Bon jour! Comme vas tu? The weather is perfect, the hotel is very French and the Parisians are being very nice this trip. I think Dvina's French helps – she's speaking very well.

Love, Joanna."

A flood of emotions raced through Torina. She had to sit. Looking at the picture she said to herself. "I could have been there too." She reflected more deeply and then other, stronger emotions came rushing back. Anger started to build again. She had felt hostility before and she knew precisely what had brought the angry scenes to mind. There had been numerous arguments and many tears: her tears. It had been painful. How could she ever think she should have been there too. Stupid! Why did she react this way? How many times did she have to put herself in this situation before she released how dumb she was? Bitch! Stupid fucking bitch, she thought to herself. That's what she was, a stupid fucking bitch. She'd never learn anything. When would she? While she adored Joanna and had wished to go to France to share the experience with her, it was her other sister Dvina was the problem, and she had gone with Joanna.

What upset Torina was her two sisters got on well together when she was not with them. Two's company and three's a crowd, they say and it is bloody well right, she thought. I'm the odd one out – the black sheep! Torina flung the postcard in the direction of the wastepaper bin. It missed and lay on the floor. She looked around the room, her space, and felt depressed. She was here in Seattle attending university and learning about logic and philosophy, while her sisters were gallivanting around France enjoying themselves. How did she do this to herself?

Almost mechanically, Torina stood and walked to the wine rack. Taking a sharp paring knife from the knife rack she rotated the bottle and cut a neat line through the cap. Changing angle she methodically lifted the metal cap and unveiled the top of the cork. She then opened a drawer and grabbed the corkscrew. Without thinking, she inserted the screw and began turning the handle at the top to force the metal screw into the cork. When it had penetrated into the cork as far as it could go she took great joy in prising the handles of the opener downwards to hear the characteristic pop of the extracted cork. She had done this many times before and effortlessly she retracted the cork from the screw, threw it into the waste bin and replaced the corkscrew in the drawer. The familiar glug-glug-glug as the first flood of red wine flowed freely from the neck of the bottle into the awaiting balloon glass. She half-filled the glass then took a large mouthful. She did not swallow immediately but held the red alcoholic fluid in her mouth to accentuate its taste, to savour the flavour and to enjoy the impact moment when it hit her throat as she finally swallowed the relaxing liquid. That's what she needed, and more the better she would feel.

Grasping the open bottle of wine in her right hand and her glass in her left, she returned to her seat on the couch. She took another large draft from her glass. Now she felt better. She started to lose the anger she had felt minutes before. Now she could reflect on her situation in a relaxed way, or it is what she convinced herself.

"That fucking Dvina," she thought. "Always giving me trouble and harassing me. For what? Just because I was her little sister. The arrogant bitch! How dare she treated me like she did." She tried to dismiss those thoughts and focus on Joanna instead.

Joanna was always nice to her. Joanna had a rare beauty although she was not beautiful to look at. She was rather plain. Her dark hair and complexion, plus simple slender body was not as attractive compared to her own blonde, buxom and shapely figure, or so Torina thought. Joanna's beauty was internal. She was deeply caring and considerate of others, particularly the infirm and lost, both animals and people. She took care of stray animals, felt sympathy for people down on their luck and loved nature, attributes Torina admired. Torina was similar, but then, several years ago she was less inclined to save starving and maltreated animals than now. Had she taken Joanna's example and incorporated it into her own personality? Maybe, but what if she had followed her sister's example. There was nothing wrong with replicating her mentor. She felt a better person for it.

Jersey Island walk

The plan for the morning was to walk along the edge of the cliff from the car park at Bouley Bay to Rozel on the Channel Island of Jersey. I had flown there from Exeter, having carried out family history research so I could visit Anne, the wife of Rodney. I first met Anne in northern Australia when she requested joining me on a rock art safari. The morning's plan was for Rodney, his surname a hyphenated tongue twister, and I to drive two cars; he leaving one at Rozel and then together we would drive to Bouley Bay to begin our walk. I drove Rod's VW Golf while Rod drove Anne's energy efficient and carbon minimal producer, a Toyota IQ. On reaching the Rozel car park and leaving Anne's car there Rod realised he had forgotten to wear hiking shoes, so we returned to the house. After changing his shoes Rod drove towards Bouley Bay, but several hundred metres up the road a working gang were repairing the road; their truck blocked the one lane road. Rod turned around and headed the other direction towards Filerty Bay.

At the bottom of the hill his phone rang and while answering it and negotiating a narrow hair-pin bend he heard his sister's voice. Caroline, the young sister of Rod was calling from London to tell him she was ill and uncertain as to whether she should fly as planned to visit them over the weekend. Rod explained to her about Anne's own recovery from intensive chemotherapy. Because Anne's immune system was vulnerable she needed to be careful about seeing people who had any contagious illness. Knowing it, Caroline had called, worried lest she might cause Anne greater health problems. Undecided, Caroline sought Rod's advice. He told her he would discuss the matter with Anne after we reached the car park; explaining where we were and what we were doing. Caroline reiterated her concerns and Rod repeated what he had explained.

We drove to the Bouley Bay car park without further incident. I took my jacket, thinking the wind might be cool, coming off the sea and rising swiftly up the cliff, even though the sun was shining and a few light clouds floated overhead. In short sleeves, Rod thought he would not be cold. The walk began with a conversation about where we were and the access track, the presence of pink and purple heather and yellow gorse.

Rod remembered about saying he would call Anne, but not having the mobile phone with him he returned to the car while I waited on the track, admiring the distant sea view. He returned with the phone and talked to Anne to find out she felt it would be fine for Caroline to visit. Anne also expressed her opinion about Caroline and whether she may have considered she was actually too ill to travel, rather than her illness affecting Anne's health. Rod and Anne discussed the issue with the outcome being a decision for Anne to leave it to Caroline to decide whether she was well enough to travel.

Rod then called Caroline to relay the message and to discuss another possible visit at Christmas instead of making the effort to fly while she did not feel well enough. They talked about it and her health, as well as Anne's condition. Rod insisted it was fine if she wanted to come as planned, but suggested she consider later in the year might be better. Caroline finally agreed to his suggestion.

We then continued our walk along an undulating and winding eroded track which gave marvellous views of the cliffs, heather, gorse and rocks bracketed by a blue sea and cloudy sky. Along the track we met five couples, several leading dogs. Nearing the end of the walk, about a half mile from where we left the first car Rod realised he had forgotten to take the key from the second car so we could drive Anne's car. We turned and headed back to the second car. I suggested he walk all the way back while I continue on and walk down into the village of Rozel to a tea house, and meet him there. He agreed and we separated on our separate courses.

I found the track and walked along the road to the seaside village of Rozel where I saw a cafe and entered. I had ordered my crab sandwich and pot of tea when I saw Rod in the car, so I waved. He saw me and parked the car before joining me in the cafe.

The crab sandwich was made with local crab and tasted plain without sauce. The tea was dark and strong and refreshing after the hour-thirty minute long walk. The dark haired waitress of Portuguese extraction told us she had just taken an apple and blackberry crumble from the oven and offered we should try it. I accepted and took cream and ice cream on the side. The crumble was delicious, and just what I needed. The large chunks of apple were too large, and should have been sliced thinner, but it was flavoursome.

After the late lunch we drove to the first car and then in both cars headed back to the house after an adventurous, aesthetic and tasteful outing.